C.

MYNA BIRD MYSTERY

Myna Bird
Mystery

PAUL BERNA

Translated from the French by
JOHN BUCHANAN-BROWN

THE BODLEY HEAD
LONDON SYDNEY
TORONTO

L'Opération Oiseau-Noir
(Paris, Éditions G.P., 1970)

Myna Bird Mystery
(London, The Bodley Head, 1970)

ISBN 0 370 01219 4
© Éditions G.P., Paris, 1970
English translation © The Bodley Head Ltd, 1970
Printed and bound in Great Britain for
The Bodley Head Ltd
9 Bow Street, London, w c 2
by C. Tinling & Co Ltd, Liverpool
Set in Photon Plantin
First published in Great Britain 1970

Contents

I

A Stout Pair of Boots

CADY GLANCED anxiously from side to side as he trudged through Mareuil with its bungalows where retired folk had their little gardens and their fierce dogs, its High Street in which nothing stirred, and its vast star of a road junction watched over by a frowning policeman. It certainly did not seem the place for a boy who had completely lost his way. Leading out of Mareuil stretched the road to Pontoise, a line of poplars on either side, a grey sky streaked by yellow smoke above. The yards and factories of the northern suburbs of Paris began to grow fewer and through the gaps in the distant walls came snatches of views which were almost rural.

On he went for another quarter of a mile or so, warily walking along the grass verge. There was little traffic apart from the lorries speeding towards Paris. Now and again the wind of their passing shook the poplars, bringing down a few more of their last remaining golden leaves. Then the lonely road returned to its autumnal silence.

The only compass Cady had was his mother-wit and the ability to keep going, acquired at a very early age by those who have to survive by their own unaided efforts. Long before he reached the corner, he was sniffing appreciatively at the familiar stench of the shanty-town hanging in the still air. The fish which the Portuguese fried and the honey-cakes which the North Africans made, scented the countryside for some distance around.

7

He slowed his pace as he came round the bend, so as to take a good look at the place. To his left there was a long grey wall on which was painted in enormous and bright red letters DEMAGNY'S WAREHOUSES. Beyond there was a gap in the wasteland, a gap torn by the bulldozers, and a forest of white pillars and scaffolding outlined against the murky sky. The hoardings said—PLASTOREX TRADING-ESTATE: *1,000 acres of factories: 10,000 new jobs. Opening 1972.* 'They've plenty of time to finish that lot,' Cady thought to himself.

Further on, behind a rickety wooden fence, he could see grimy brick buildings and piles of scrap-metal; then the junction with the road to Epinay, while the vista ended in the distance with the railway embankment curving sweetly across the horizon.

Cady crossed the road and slowly retraced his steps, peering in the other direction through the poplars. The shanty-town lay in a gently-sloping hollow surrounded by bushes and saplings battered by the November storms. The gipsies, having been there longest, had their caravans and big American cars parked in the best spot, leaving the homeless with their hordes of children to make what they could of the mire. Shacks made of planks, corrugated iron or tarpaper, leaned against one another like flimsy houses of cards on either side of a muddy track sprinkled with clinker. Cady felt better when he saw a mob of some fifty young ragamuffins rush shrieking through this wretched village. He left the road and walked slowly down a muddy path leading to the nearest hovels. Then he halted and, as custom demanded, stood well in view. There was nothing to show that they would accept him, so he was all ready to beat a rapid retreat under a hail of stones.

Sandra spotted him on her way back from Bofano's grocery. She had her gang with her and the Casbah gang as well, a lively lot, a dozen or so all told, who ruled the roost at Bois-Bréau when their fathers were out at work.

'Hi!' she said to the others. 'I smell strangers. Any of you seen him around before?'

'Can't say I have,' Simbad answered. 'Could have run away from Petit-Colombes.'

Slowly and silently they approached, staring suspiciously at the intruder. Over a moth-eaten sweater, Cady wore an ancient reddish woollen jerkin which came halfway down his legs. On his feet were almost brand-new wellingtons, but one was black and the other dull red, while the right boot was plainly two sizes larger than the left. His tangled shock of fair hair fell over a pair of eyes as bright and sharp as a puppy's.

He stood his ground and tried to look unconcerned while the others closed in on him. This group was no different from the other ragamuffins he had met on his travels. Children in the shanty-towns are the same wherever you go and all speak the same private language. This particular group muttered and seemed to wait on the decision of the brown-haired girl who stood a head taller than the rest of them.

'What do you want?' Sandra asked.

Cady had no reason for not telling the truth.

'Nothing very much. Just a bite to eat and somewhere dry to sleep.'

His frankness made them all grin.

'Same old story,' Sandra said. 'After a year's up, you'll still be knocking around with one family or another . . . Run away from home?'

'Never had one.'

'Well, you must have come from somewhere,' Simbad retorted as he stared at the newcomer's odd boots.

'I was at Moulin-Noir, on the other side of the Seine. A good spot. Nobody bothered you. But the land was going up in value and the council wanted it back. So the fuzz turned up this morning in full force with buses to take away anyone who wouldn't go quietly. In the end, everyone went off in different directions and the people who were looking after me just left me in the mad rush to get away.'

'That's what we expect here one of these days,' Sandra sighed. 'And all because of the Mangler.'

She pointed to the fence and barbed-wire round the scrap-metal yard opposite the shanty-town.

'You'll always get your Mangler,' Cady agreed. 'The one in Moulin-Noir shot cats and rolled the drunks on a Saturday night.'

This remark removed any last suspicions which may have lingered round the stranger. They had still to take him into their family, but they recognised him as one of themselves. He stared approvingly at the Wild Western style village with its potholed main street flanked by duckboard sidewalks and houses built of cardboard and corrugated iron.

'Never heard of this place of yours before.'

'Bois-Bréau,' said Sandra. 'As you can see, it's not exactly heaven.'

'Where's the wood?' Cady asked, peering in all directions.

'That went up in smoke the first winter we were here. All that's left is the patch of bushes where we play in the summer. The trees you can see over there behind the Casbah belong to Saint-Adrien, an old cemetery they still use. But no one would dare lay a finger on them . . . We aren't quite as bad as that . . . What's your name?'

'Cady.'

'That's not a surname,' said Sandra. 'It's not a Christian name either.'

'I can't help that. That's what I've always been called.'

10

The tall girl with the brown hair spoke kindly and there was nothing false about her smile.

'Well, chum, we'd like to help, but you'll have to pay for your supper at least . . . Got any money?'

'Not a bean,' Cady admitted. 'And I hadn't had a bite to eat when I left Moulin-Noir.'

All the same he turned out the pockets of his jerkin and produced an old ball-point pen, a police-whistle, a ping-pong ball, two dusty toffees, an aluminium coffee-spoon, a clothes-peg, a lighter without a flint, a Red Indian who had lost his right arm and a toy car which had lost its wheels, three coupons giving a special reduction on some brand of detergent, an incomplete pack of cards done up in an elastic band, and the knight from an imitation ivory chess set. This treasure he munificently gave away to the younger children clustered around Sandra. The four older boys stood a little to one side, apparently unimpressed by this display of generosity.

The boy called Simbad, however, seemed unable to take his eyes off the odd pair of boots which the stranger wore. Utter amazement covered his swarthy face.

'You going to give me your boots?' he snapped.

This was no simple question and Cady understood at once.

'They're the only ones I've got. How do you think I'll manage without any?'

He looked round to see if the brown-haired girl would stand up for him, but Sandra was looking away and seemed in no hurry to come to his aid. Boots were no business of hers.

Slowly Cady took one step back and then another, a fixed grin hiding his anxiety.

'Come off it!' he mouthed. 'You don't think I'm going walking the streets barefoot in the rain?'

He had not expected so sudden an attack. The bigger

11

boys were on him in a flash, had him flat on his back in the mud and clinker and, purring with excitement but without hurting him more than was absolutely necessary, whipped off his wellingtons. Simbad immediately put on the right boot, his brother, Ali, the left.

'Just our size! Couldn't have found better in a shop. Look at us, we're proper toffs!'

Everyone hooted with laughter as Cady heaved himself up on one elbow, hiding the misery in his eyes. He had been in some tough spots in Moulin-Noir and one or two other places between Nanterre and La Garenne where the homeless lived. But no one had gone so far as to steal his shirt or his food. What was more, with winter almost here, a good pair of boots was of vital importance.

Scornfully Simbad and Ali tossed their old boots to him, boots with toes which gaped at him like the horrid jaws of a pike.

'Keep them yourself,' he said politely. 'I'd rather use my own feet.'

His foot-cloths had come adrift in the struggle and he refastened them before he got to his feet, still keeping watch on the others out of the corner of his eye. The younger boys and girls were expecting more presents from this heaven-sent simpleton. Simbad and his friends still sniggered, while Sandra watched with a nasty, calculating look in her eye.

'That jerkin he's wearing is far too long,' she said at last. 'It's half way down his legs. It's good cloth too, and it's got real leather strengthening . . . I heard old Garcia wants to trade his sheepskin coat. I wonder if we couldn't do a deal.'

One or two doors along the smoky main street had opened and fierce-looking housewives in their aprons looked out, disturbed by sounds of the argument. Cady delayed no longer and made off up the muddy track. At the top there was more traffic about, lorries making for Paris with a rush and a roar. Dusk was closing in and there could be no more than an hour of daylight left. It was unthinkable that he should try to go back all the long way he had come that day, back to Mareuil and a Moulin-Noir cleared by the police. Cady would rather keep pressing on.

He crossed the road at once to escape the muggers of Bois-Bréau. The railway embankment far away to the north looked attractive. It was bound to lead to sidings in which unserviceable wagons stood in their retirement. If you were careful, you could sleep warm and dry for weeks without being disturbed by the yard foremen, who were often worse than the police about little things like sleeping rough.

Five hundred yards away, the road dived under a bridge. He made for it along the left-hand strip of verge. The grass was wet and this, and the mud which his foot-cloths had soaked up at Bois-Bréau, made him squelch along like a duck. He did not look round as he passed the last gate, opening on a desert of rusty scrap.

'Happy journey, son,' a voice from the darkness growled. 'But you won't get very far without your slippers!'

'I left them with the neighbours,' Cady answered in a desperate effort to be cheerful. 'There were twelve or thirteen of them—four to pull my boots off and the rest to cheer. . . . I won't forget Bois-Bréau quickly, I can tell you!'

'You couldn't fight back?'

'What with? I'd been on my feet all day, without a bite to eat. The fuzz in a patrol car chased me all the way to Mareuil. They didn't catch me—they didn't even see me—that's not bad in a built-up area. I just stopped to get my breath back and before I knew what was happening a couple of tricksters had pinched the boots off my feet.'

'You went to the wrong address, that's all.'

Cady moved over to the gateway without any real hope of a miracle taking place. Grown-ups usually slip you some money as they hurry past, but that's all. They do not want to be involved with homeless children, who cause too much trouble.

Despite a four or five days' growth of beard, the burly man standing behind the bars of the gate had a not unkindly face and there was a twinkle in his eyes. He wore a short yellow oilskin coat, a pair of grease-stained blue overalls and thick, elbow-length leather gloves.

'I'd like to help,' he added staring down at Cady's feet, 'but you'll have to be careful. Once I've got the gate open, you follow me over to that shed on the right, and keep out of sight behind me.'

He lit a cigarette and turned to look into the yard. Across the open muddy space came a tractor, slowly towing a trailer laden with scrap-metal. Over to the left, more men in yellow oilskins worked a hydraulic press with gaping jaws which gave a sinister creak as they reduced the scrap to square parcels of metal. In the background stood a two-storey brick building, the lights from its windows gleaming in the dusk.

'Let's go,' the man whispered. 'Now's the time. Make yourself as small as you can and stick right behind me.'

He opened the gate a fraction of an inch and then strolled lazily over to the nearest shed, skirting the walls of the office, shadowed by the slim shape of Cady at his heels. At last they reached the corner of the shed. The scrap-worker signalled to the boy and pushed the door. It rumbled as it opened.

'Quick! In you go and choose what you want. I'll stop outside to see the coast's clear . . . '

Cady's eyes widened as he went into the gloom. The far wall of the shed was hidden behind a mountain of cartons

14

torn open to allow their contents to tumble out and partly cover the floor. There must have been a thousand pairs of boots of all sizes, black, white and red, matt or shiny, most of them felt-lined into the bargain. It was a regular treasure-house! In frenzied haste he tried on one pair after the other.

'Found a pair to fit you?' a voice growled from outside. 'Hurry up, or I'll lock you in.'

Cady came out in his new footwear, nervously banging his heels and bending his knees to test the comfort of his new acquisition. They were a splendid pair of supple rubber boots, their deep tan shade imitating leather, a top quality product with the label *Made in Italy*. He could not have done better.

'Happy?'

The boy stammered his thanks.

'Go in front of me, and I shouldn't run if I were you. If the boss sees you, he'll kick you out of the gate.'

But they got across the yard without any bother and Cady slipped through the gate like a wraith.

'Keep your mouth shut,' the man said, when he had closed the gate and lit the stub of his cigarette once more. 'Don't you tell your mates where you got those boots from or I'll be out of a job . . . '

For a moment or two they stared at one another through the bars, each appreciating the humour of the situation.

'Where are you going to kip down tonight?'

'Haven't a clue!' Cady laughed in answer. 'Anyway it doesn't matter so much now.'

He exhibited his new boots and stamped cheerfully on the soggy ground. The man was still curious.

'What's your name?'

'Cady. It's easy to remember.'

'Where do your parents live?'

15

'Never had any. But I can get by all right without them.'

'All the same it's sad to hear someone say so!' The kind-hearted scrap-worker sighed. 'Now listen, son, if you're ever really on your beam-ends, come this way and look out for me. My name's Philippon.'

'I shan't forget that,' Cady assured him.

They paused for a moment before they parted. Philippon looked up and down the road as if he were measuring the distance, and then stared at the young wanderer.

'Which way are you going now?'

Cady did not disappoint his benefactor. There was no hesitation. He cut across the road and bravely headed for the shanty-town.

In the meantime the gang had changed their field of action. Boys and girls were chasing one another round a long, low, wooden hut, painted dark green, standing at the end of the village street a little way behind the line of hovels. A big, shaggy dog leaped from one to the other in pursuit of a football made of old rags which they were kicking with all their might, sending up showers of mud and clinker. Suddenly one of them spotted the boy and their game came to an abrupt end. The dog snatched the opportunity to pounce on the ball which he dropped at Cady's feet. He then sniffed the boy's legs, his tail wagging in friendship.

'You again?' Sandra said in a patient voice.

'I expect he's come to ask us if we'd like his jerkin,' Simbad exclaimed and made them all laugh. 'The fifth time he leaves us, our mate will be down to his shirt.'

Cady approached them smiling, poking out first his left leg and then his right so that they could all see his new boots gleaming in the twilight.

'See those?' he said.

Simbad stared at them in surprise.

'Cor! They look as if they've just come out of a shop.'

'That's right,' said Cady. 'Now you try and take them off me!'

His challenge produced silence. The smaller ones began sensibly to edge away. The dog picked up the rag ball and began to worry it as he looked around for someone to play with. In front of Cady no one moved.

'Trying to scare us?' Sandra muttered.

'No. I came back because I'm hungry. And anyway I don't mean to sleep in the wet grass if I can help it. There must be something wrong with you if we can't work out an arrangement between us. But if we can't, I'll be off to Argenteuil or Sartrouville.' He spoke quietly, without spite or bitterness. Simultaneously the young Algerians from Bois-Bréau, Sandra and the youngsters in the background all accepted him. The smallest of them all, Pimpin Léonard, gravely expressed his opinion.

'The best thing we can do is put him in the old hut the Portuguese cleared out of. I know it hasn't got a door, but the four walls are still standing.'

'What are you talking about!' Simbad roared with laughter. 'It's full of fleas and dead rats. He might as well spend the night under a railway bridge.'

'The main thing,' Sandra said, 'is to keep it dark from the old folk. If they've got another mouth to feed, you'll be able to hear them yell the other side of Paris. Mine might put up with him for a day or two, but no longer. And what are we going to do after that?'

'Wait and see,' Cady answered. 'As far as I'm concerned the main thing is to get my foot in the door.'

Thereupon they unanimously made him their friend.

'I suppose there must be a hundred of us kids in Bois-Bréau,' Sandra explained. 'But our gang's the best run, and you needn't worry about the others; the gipsies

17

keep themselves to themselves and the Portuguese are always at one another's throats.'

It was getting dark. The tall lamp-standards shone at intervals along the road and their glare blotted out the last low gleams of sunset. By now lights began to glimmer along the street through the cellophane or oil-paper windows.

'We call it our Champs-Elysées,' Sandra joked. 'It's got a drugstore and a night-club.'

A whistle shrilled from behind Demagny's Warehouses and a little later came the stumble of feet down the street.

'Here come our dads,' said Simbad.

Cady watched the weary, muddy workers come down the street of Bois-Bréau in silent groups. Most of them were labourers, the unimportant people who worked the cement-mixers, laid the bricks and fixed the beams and shuttering, the lowest-paid workers who strained their muscles all day long at the toughest jobs. And because they all did much the same work, they finished up by looking much the same, whatever country they had come from originally.

The nightly homecoming was the only thing that broke up the gang, each to his wretched hovel in the shanty-town: the Algerians to the south, the Spaniards and the Portuguese alongside Saint-Adrien's cemetery; in the middle, facing Demagny's Warehouses, the French and a scattering of Italians, and the pandemonium where the stateless people, the out-of-work and the hunted-looking prisoners on licence forgathered; beyond that, on the edge of what had been the Bois-Bréau, the village of cardboard and canvas where the half-starved Negroes lived; and finally to the north the wagon-lines of the gipsies, a strongly-protected circle of caravans parked end-to-end.

Cady left the bulk of the gang and followed Sandra and her young brother Mimile halfway down the murky street.

The workers were pouring into a wooden hut. Its bright lights had suddenly been switched on to drive the darkness from this part of the village.

'That's the canteen,' Sandra explained. 'They sell beer and wine, and spirits outside working hours. Fat Théo runs it—he's one of the Mangler's strong-arm men—and he rakes in the profits from there too. The men who don't drink—and we've still got some who don't—called that boozer the "Eldorado" for a joke. Opposite is Bofano's grocery. The Italian's okay. He'll let you have something to eat on tick. Well, what do you think of our little holiday camp?'

'It's not as bad as all that,' Cady admitted. 'I'm not sorry I left Moulin-Noir. All you got there were crooks and dead-beats; at least people work here.'

She dragged him down a narrow alley leading to the last tattered bushes left in Bois-Bréau. The shack on the end to the right was built of wooden packing-cases and had only one glass-less window sawn out of the front wall. Through the asbestos sheeted roof poked a long stove-pipe held up by wire stays. A rich smell of cooking drifted out of the half-open door.

'Mashed potatoes, cabbage and rhinoceros stew,' Sandra announced. 'It's not a bad mixture, except sometimes the meat's none too good. A lion wouldn't touch it when it's raw, but if you can manage to get it down, it'll keep you going until dinner-time tomorrow. Follow us and don't worry. The old woman does get steamed up sometimes.'

Cady came in shyly behind them. It was a room some twelve by fifteen feet, with blackened walls, lit by a butane gas lamp hung between two joists. At the far end a little grey-haired woman was bent over a coal-range, stirring a saucepan with one hand and with the other putting mincemeat into a frying-pan.

'Oh! Gran, we've brought back a mate of ours,' Sandra gaily called. 'You'll like him, his name's Cady.'

'Out!' said Madame Rouvier, not even turning round.

She had scarcely raised her voice. Back came Sandra boldly to the attack.

'He's come from Moulin-Noir, just imagine that? He's all skin and bone.'

The old lady went on stirring her rhinoceros stew.

'Out!' was all she said in a slightly louder voice.

'He won't eat much,' Sandra continued to plead. 'Only half a plate. Then, just for tonight, he could sleep beside Mimile. The blanket's big enough.'

'Out!' bellowed Madame Rouvier.

This time her order rolled like thunder round the shack. Awe-struck, Cady backed towards the door but was pushed back into the room again by an old man who came limping through the doorway.

'Can't get rid of this sciatica,' he groaned. 'I've only to get a couple of wet or foggy days and I'm laid up. If Léonard hadn't given me a hand, I'd never have got through the day.'

He put his lunch-box on the table and wearily took off his yellow oilskin coat. His jaws were lean and rough with a white stubble, his body long and thin, his arms clumsy from a lifetime of being asked to do more than they were able. He blinked in the lamplight before he suddenly became aware that there was a third child.

'Where's this come from?'

At last Madame Rouvier turned away from the stove. Cady was dreading that she would prove to be another of those termagants whom he had seen in the village street. But she was just a spiritless little woman with a pasty, impassive face, barely warmed by her brief burst of anger. Something seemed to be the matter with her eyes, for they were red-rimmed and never stopped watering.

'Sandrine and Mimile brought him back,' she whined. 'The day before yesterday it was a cat with a broken leg; last week it was a little flea-bitten girl the Portuguese had been beating; the day after tomorrow they'll pick up some drunk from outside the canteen and install him in our best bed. I don't know what we can do about it.'

The patriarch of the Plastorex building-site breathed deeply.

'Out you go! My earnings will feed four and no more. Five is one too many!'

Cady went out into the dark and the cold, snuffed the breeze and came back in almost at once. He was beginning to like the Rouviers' palatial premises.

'Do you want my boot in your backside?' the old man asked him roughly.

'Keep calm,' Cady retorted coolly. 'I can pay for my board and lodging, you know.'

'Got some money, then?'

'Something better than that. Give me your hand, don't get all tensed up, just relax. I shan't hurt you, I'm not big enough or strong enough.'

The gas lamp flared as bright as ever, but the atmosphere in the shack seemed to get warmer. Apprehensively Monsieur Rouvier put out a gnarled and massive fist. Cady's slim, smooth fingers skimmed over it, closed like a vice over the hairy wrist and then slowly but steadily began to twist it. At first the old man tried to resist, but then his body was sharply swung over to the left. He put out his leg to regain his balance and as he did so he gave a shout. The longstanding pain which had tormented him all day had vanished in a flash, leaving him with a satisfying sense of well-being.

'You've just performed a miracle,' he gasped.

'It's only a bone-setter's trick,' Cady answered shyly. 'For a couple of years I lived with a crazy old girl who

21

used to treat labourers, engine-drivers and pneumatic-drill operators. It's all in the hands, but you must add a little something extra to make your patients perk up.'

He looked up and the Rouviers were won over by his grin.

'You'll be staying with us?' the old man asked.

'You bet,' Cady answered. 'If you all want me . . . '

The old lady with the watering eyes set a fifth plate at the greasy table. The room was filled with the delicious smell of rhinoceros stew. Sandra and her little brother seemed hypnotized by their guest. First of all there were the brand-new boots, which seemed to have arrived from nowhere, and now the old man was skipping round the shack as though he had forgotten his sciatica. It was miraculous!

Madame Rouvier had not stinted the stew-pot. There were second helpings all round and Cady went to bed happy. Soon after midnight he was wakened by a cat crawling over the children to find a comfortable corner. Once he had found a place, the creature began to purr happily. In the end the noise got on the boy's nerves and he looked up and listened.

Every now and then the embers in the range would glow in a gust of wind and cast a reddish light on the dusty floor. At the other end of the room the old couple snored behind a blanket hung on a clothes line. Next to it Sandra slept in a camp-bed in the darkest corner.

There was no catch on the door and the wind made it creak and bang against its rickety frame. Cady stared past it, out into the dank and silent darkness. He was taking stock of his new domain—the endless wall round Demagny's Warehouses, the fence surrounding the Mangler's scrap-yard, the huge gap in the wastelands from which rose the towers of the Plastorex trading-estate, and finally the huddle of shacks and crude shelters called Bois-Bréau.

2

The Mangler

MADAME MEUNIER was usually the first to arrive, driving her antiquated 2 CV which bucked and ground its way over the bumpy track. The first thing she did was to open the doors of the house painted dark green —Monsieur Langelin had been able to buy the paint at a massive discount—and then she toured the shanty-town to collect the complaints of the good ladies standing in their doorways. The children gave warning of her approach with shrill whistles and easily eluded her in the maze of the town built of packing cases.

Only the very smallest would let her take them by the hand and lead them to the Green House, would gravely accept her little kindnesses, allow her to wipe their noses or wash their ears, and would then sit themselves down on the benches to await the arrival of the man they called their Guardian Angel, who usually appeared on the scene on the stroke of ten. As soon as they heard the stutter of his scooter coming down the slope their faces turned hungrily towards the door. He always brought them something—picture books, sweets or biscuits, games and toys which he himself had put together and clumsily painted, and, best of all, a gentle smile which the children of Bois-Bréau saw all too seldom on the haggard faces of their fathers.

Monsieur Langelin's forehead and hollow cheeks still bore the marks of the beatings he had taken when trying to relieve the homeless from Nanterre to Gennevilliers, but nothing could upset his cheerfulness or divert him from his work.

Once he had handed out his presents amid joyous confusion, he would gather the bigger children in front of the blackboard to teach them a few letters more, sometimes a whole word, would flash pieces of cardboard at them and get them to repeat in chorus the numbers painted on them, or would organise a sing-song to the accompaniment of his out-of-tune guitar.

The last fifteen minutes were the most interesting. All became quiet once more while he told, simply and without moralizing or sentimentality, the story of a man who had lived two thousand years ago in the Middle East. It was a wonderful adventure story, episode following breath-taking episode, with a mounting excitement of which the Early Christian Fathers would not have disapproved. He had the happy knack of making the characters come to life with such realism that the simpler souls among his listeners began to think that their friend was modestly disguising the story of his own life in this way.

The age of miracles had still to reach Bois-Bréau. Monsieur Langelin thought himself lucky all the same to have found a dozen stout fellows who put up this promised shelter for the children, although the wilder element among them often deserted it. In any case his helpers had had to yield to the threats of the Scrap-metal King and had lent their aid on one condition—that the building should be used as a school and not as a chapel. Because of this the Green House did not even have a cross on its façade.

Old man Rouvier yawned as he opened the door and glanced outside. It was still quite dark. A thick mist from the Seine had closed in on them, muffling the noise of the lorries which had by now started to run along the road.

You could just make out their yellow headlights at the junction of Croix-Souci, which grew brighter as they turned the corner and then gradually faded in the fog.

'If your sciatica comes back,' the old lady grunted from her place by the stove, 'don't you be obstinate. Just drop your tools. I'd rather you lost a day's pay than have you brought home on a stretcher.'

Gingerly the old man tried out his left leg, bending it and kicking out sharply. But he did not feel the slightest twinge of pain. Reassured, his interest in the miracle-worker revived. The two boys were sleeping like dormice with the blanket drawn up to their ears. The magician's over-abundant mop of fair hair worried Monsieur Rouvier.

'We've never had fleas in our house and I don't want to get infested like those filthy pigs over in the southern side who only take a bath when the rain comes through on to their beds. You tell Sandra to take the boy to Madame Meunier. And see she goes this morning and not in a week's time.'

He put on his yellow oilskins, picked up his lunch-box and joined the other beasts of burden who walked in silence towards the Plastorex site.

An hour later, when the three children poked their noses outside, it was barely light and the mist was just as thick. You could not even see the wall of Demagny's Warehouses on the other side of the road.

'Let's go down to the Casbah,' Sandra decided. 'The Boubarkas and their mates will be waiting for us.'

'I don't need an army to take me to get my hair cut,' Cady observed.

Little Mimile chuckled.

'Round here we go about in a gang. That's the way we always do it. You can wander about on your own if you like, but sooner or later the Mangler's toughs will be on you like a ton of bricks. They'll have the boots off your feet and the shirt off your back, and knock a few of your teeth out into the bargain.'

First they picked up the Italians who lived in the alley, Beppo Torrente and his sister Fina, and then little Pimpin Léonard, who was on watch at the corner of the street and whom Sandra took under her wing. A few shivering figures were waiting outside Bofano's grocery for the milk to come, while opposite the lights of the canteen glared through the mist.

As he followed his new friends, Cady noticed the dull roar of rushing water and the occasional gurgle coming from somewhere down in the village.

'That's the huge waste-pipe from the Radam Works,' Sandra explained. 'One day last summer Monsieur Boubarka, Simbad and Ali's father, took the trouble to shift a bit of the casing and now we've got main drainage. It's quite straightforward, we dump all our rubbish down the hole and the waste from the factory washes it away almost at once. But don't you go falling in if you're round this way. You'll land up half a mile away in the Seine under the barges by Maisons-Laffitte . . . And this is the Wadi Radam!'

Cady saw the piece of broken casing lying surrounded by filth, and the gloomy pit from which came a sulphurous stench. Nimble figures danced on the brink as they tipped in the contents of their buckets and bins. In shanty-towns this job is left to those who contribute nothing to the family wages, and the children of Bois-Bréau did it uncomplainingly, even in bad weather.

Beppo whistled to warn their friends in the southern quarter that they were there, and soon they came swarming out of their tumbledown hovels, some little better than chicken-huts. There were Saïd Boubarka, known as Simbad, his younger brother, Ali, and their cousins Taïeb

26

and Mourab, all four dressed in faded jeans and men's jackets with the sleeves cut down to fit them.

They differed little from the others except for their darker complexion, blacker eyes, which twinkled wickedly, and an air of laziness about them which they only shook off when they needed to use their legs or their fists to get them out of trouble. They accepted Alexandrine Rouvier's moral leadership, for they were clever enough to realise that they had a far freer hand in the village and could get away with a great deal more than they would have done but for the cover provided by someone with her energy and gift of the gab.

This villainous crew was not particularly surprised to discover that Sandra had taken the newcomer in tow.

'Slept in your boots, eh?' Simbad asked him and stared dreamily at the marvellous objects.

'There aren't any thieves in the Rouviers' place,' Cady retorted drily.

'You ought to give us the address of the shop,' said Mourab, 'then we could all get a pair.'

Cady bore no grudges.

'It's a secret, but once yours start letting in the water, I promise I'll try to get a pair to fit you.'

Sandra counted to see how many of her friends were there, not to reckon their fighting strength, but to make sure nobody had been left behind.

'We'll pick up the Belin sisters as we go past the canteen,' she said. 'Has anyone seen César?'

'The Negro's waiting for us at the top of the Champs-Elysées,' Taïeb answered. 'You can guess why?'

'Another fight with the gipsies?'

'Come off it. He's keeping an eye on the cross-roads, because of all this fog. The first sign of trouble and Mahmadou'll come and warn us.'

They walked up the muddy street keeping a wary eye

open. It was a long time since they had had to meet an open challenge, but nobody wanted a handful of filth in the face, thrown from the shelter of some dark alley. The best whistler in the gang, Beppo, trilled like a chaffinch as they approached Bofano's grocery and out of a cramped tar-paper hovel came two fair-haired little girls each encased in an old woollen coat. Violet and Rose joined the gang. Madame Belin herself could only tell which twin was which by the coloured ribbons in their hair, and they were suspected of sometimes swapping this identity mark to confuse their friends.

'I hope you've all had something to eat?' Sandra asked.

She was rather inclined to make a martyr of herself over her friends' diet, and often some of them were too ashamed to admit that the crust of bread they had demanded as an extra went into the family larder.

'All we had was a cup of tea with no milk in it and a piece of toast half the size of my hand,' Ali Boubarka announced. 'Mum owes Bofano for a fortnight's bread and she doesn't dare show her face in the shop. So we're waiting for pay-day.'

'We'll take a little trip round to the Green House first of all,' said Sandra. 'We'll try and cadge a packet of biscuits off the Guardian Angel. Come on!'

Fat Théo, muffled in a sheepskin jacket, was talking in a lordly way to a pair of down-and-outs in front of his dive. Wisely the children gave him a wide berth, for he was more likely in his pleasant way to wish you good-day with the toe of his boot.

'He threatened to turn us out and burn the place down yesterday,' said Beppo Torrente. 'And when you think we pay a hundred francs' rent for a few rotten wooden boards.'

'That's the regular price in the northern end of the village,' Sandra sighed. 'Nobody owns the land, but the

28

Mangler got his men to put in the foundations and run in the two water-pipes, and having done that he can squeeze what he likes out of poor folk.'

'Whatever you say, Théo doesn't dare come into the Casbah on his own now,' said Simbad. 'Someone I know said he'd chuck him head first down the Wadi Radam.'

'He's too fat,' Pimpin exclaimed and made them laugh. 'He'd block the hole.'

Madame Meunier had left the door ajar to tempt in anyone who might be lingering on the threshold. Accompanied by Monsieur Langelin's bass, innocent treble voices at the other end of the building announced:

'The-ba-ker-bakes-good-bread . . . '

'And old Bofano sells it at twice the price you'd pay anywhere else,' Mimile Rouvier muttered as he came in after his big sister.

The social worker smiled at the newcomers and signed for them to come over to her table. In her nurse's white coat she seemed so puny, almost deformed, with an unattractive air and a nose that was too big and beaky for her face, a feature which had earned her many an unkind nickname at the outset. However, her tormenters were soon silenced when they met the warmth of her eyes and felt the gentle touch of her hand on the thousands of cuts and bruises which were the daily harvest of the jungle of Bois-Bréau.

'Somebody ill?' she asked.

'No,' said Sandra. 'We've just come about our mate's hair. Grand-dad reckons he's got fleas in it, and if he comes home with this mop still on, the old man'll chuck him out of the house.'

The boy peered from behind her. Madame Meunier's smile faded. One more to prove his worth or lack of it. Where had he come from, anyway? Apart from a pair of brand-new boots, the newcomer was nothing to write home about.

'What's your name?'

'Cady . . .'

Madame Meunier looked down to hide her surprise.

'Someone over at Gennevilliers was telling me about you,' she said softly. 'And how's old Augustine keeping?'

'Died during the summer,' Cady answered without expression. 'She wasn't as old as all that, not much more than seventy, but the folk she'd cured for nothing just let her starve to death in her shack. I managed to find a place after that behind the Saint-Gobain works over in Moulin-Noir; it wasn't too damp and there were some working-people living there too. And then, yesterday morning, the fuzz arrived without a word of a warning. They gave everyone an hour to clear out and take their stuff off in their old bangers or on their hand-carts and then they started an orphan hunt. The cops searched every single hut that was still standing, but luckily I knew what they were up to and I slipped through them.'

While he kept one eye on the children sitting round the blackboard, Monsieur Langelin had fixed the other on the escaper and strained to catch what he was saying. He was one of a thousand tough little animals who somehow survive their lack of any family-ties whatsoever. Slipping through any social security net, they move from one slum to another, swapping their rags and tatters when they feel like it, putting on a few inches in height, thin- or plump-cheeked depending upon their neighbours' circumstances: the only thing they can call their own a first name and the glimmering of a surname lost in the mystery of their birth . . . Such was Cady.

'Come and sit on this bench,' Madame Meunier said as she picked up her scissors and clippers.

The boy did not object to what she did with his head

and under the fascinated gaze of his friends she had clipped the tangled mass in a few minutes.

'Find any?' asked a little voice in the back row.

The question made them all snigger.

'Not a single one,' Madame Meunier replied.

'They don't find my skin very tasty,' Cady admitted. 'Anyway, that's all you pick up if you live on air.'

His cynical remark revived the visitors' anxiety and more than one of them glanced hungrily towards the carton in which their Guardian Angel kept the gifts which Providence bestowed upon him.

'You aren't going to play outside all morning in this fog?' Madame Meunier asked them anxiously. 'Stay here until the sun starts to break through. Monsieur Langelin's stories won't give you brain fever.'

'We've heard them all before,' Pimpin Léonard muttered from the rear.

'Right, then you can tell one for him, and your friends will enjoy it twice as much. Would you like a hot drink to help you?'

A large saucepan of milk was warming on the oil-stove in her surgery. This emboldened Sandra.

'We couldn't have something to eat?' she asked. 'The Boubarkas are half-starved.'

Madame Meunier looked enquiringly towards her confederate. He answered almost at once.

'A bar of chocolate for each of the toddlers,' he said as he opened his treasure chest. 'The older children can have a slice of bread with a bit of sausage on it. That's all I can manage this morning. Each take your turn please, and no pushing or shoving.'

Boys and girls leaped over the benches in a wild rush for the far end of the room. Animal cries rose above the din as the rations were handed out.

Her wan face lit by some inner glow, Madame Meunier

31

put out the cups and shared her malted milk among the children of Bois-Bréau. She could not draw the older children to this shelter nor keep them there as a duty, without the risk of destroying the imperfect attraction which the Green House held for these young savages. She had to tame them very gently by the occasional treat. Most of them took the bread and milk, not as their due, but as if it were the present of some invisible host whose name they dared not utter. Some of them said a shy thank-you, eyes fixed upon the hand which fed them, thank-you being a noble word which finds little place in the ungracious language of the shanty-town. Monsieur Langelin listened as the words dropped now and then like a short but heart-felt prayer.

'Thank you!' Cady exclaimed loudly as he took the piece of bread and the sausage.

His eyes met those of his benefactor glinting with kind-hearted curiosity.

'How old are you?' Monsieur Langelin asked.

'Round twelve or thirteen: can't be much more. But I can read and write and count. Old Augustine taught me in her spare time.'

'And before that?'

'I've forgotten. It's so long ago . . . '

Monsieur Langelin nodded.

'I'm sure the old lady has gone to her reward in Heaven. All the same she'd have been more sensible if she'd gone into an old people's home and left you with a decent family.'

'With that riff-raff at Gennevilliers, are you joking? Nobody would have had me. At the finish, every time I went round to get her fees from her patients as likely as not I'd get a beating instead. They said her mattress was stuffed with banknotes. A likely tale! The only thing she left me were her secrets, and that's something. I know how to put back a slipped disc and cure sprains and wrenches.'

'Do you indeed?' Monsieur Langelin said disbelievingly. 'How nice to have a healer in our midst. At all events you won't be short of patients in Bois-Bréau.'

'He's telling the truth,' little Mimile interrupted. 'Grand-dad came home last night with his sciatica. And do you know what? Cady cured him in a flash, by making him hop around on one leg. It was a miracle. Even Gran stood by the stove with eyes like cart-wheels.'

When the laughter had died down, their Guardian Angel in the grey sweater made the bigger children sit down behind the little ones.

'I'm only too pleased to give up my place to our friend Pimpin. Now, let's have a story from him.'

'Any one you like!' Beppo shouted. 'Give us the loaves and fishes first. I don't really believe it, but it's nice to hear of those half-starved beggars making out, thanks to the Holy Spirit.'

Crimson with pride, Pimpin stood in front of the blackboard and began his tale. He stuck to the letter of the Gospel story until his memory let him down and then he went on by setting the Mangler on the track of this Jesus and rescuing the latter in the nick of time with the help of the labourers of Bois-Bréau. This was taking things a little too far. Madame Meunier laughed until she cried, while their Guardian Angel clapped his hands to stop the arguments. Luckily a muffled explosion rattled the rickety windows of the Green House and the hubbub was stilled at once.

Cady, who was modestly sitting in the back row, heard someone come pounding full tilt down the corridor leading to the class-room. The door was flung open with a bang and there on the threshold stood the spectral figure of the gang's look-out man. His skeletal form was draped

33

in a flowing army great-coat, and he wore a pink knitted Balaclava helmet which left only a tiny portion of his black face exposed and his great eyes rolling in excitement.

'Up to the cross-roads, everybody!' shrilled César Mahmadou. 'A huge Belgian lorry's just run into Demagny's breakdown truck! Mates, that lorry was stacked with spuds! There's a couple of tons of good honest spuds all over the road! The gipsies are shovelling them up already! Bring your sacks, bring your baskets, bring your hand-carts and let's go! There'll be enough for everyone. But get a move on and clear the lot before the fuzz gets there.'

Monsieur Langelin raised his arms to heaven: Madame Meunier tried to stop them; both were ineffective. Cady was borne away in the rush and the next thing he knew he was outside hot on Simbad's heels, the latter neck-and-neck with his brother who was a whisker behind Sandra. Mourab and Taïeb were in hot pursuit, while Mimile, Pimpin and the twins brought up the rear, their little legs going for all they were worth. Nobody was going to doubt this miraculous draught of potatoes which the fog had brought them.

A narrow track between high banks skirted the gipsies' encampment and came out just below the Croix-Souci cross-roads. Fog reduced visibility to twenty feet, but the potatoes were still rolling gaily down the slope and bouncing to a halt in the wet grass. Nobody had been killed in the accident, as was easy to guess from the heated exchange between the two drivers, who had scrambled out of their wrecked lorries.

Not wishing to lose an ounce of this windfall, Sandra at once called to the leader of the gipsies' gang, Zalko.

'Here, chum, let's fight it out another day. What we've got to do now is stash away these windfall spuds. Counting the kids, we're each twelve or thirteen strong, so let's organise a salvage squad as fast as we can, get the spuds down to the end of the road and when we've got them there we can split them between us . . . Agreed?'

Even now the sirens of the police-cars were wailing in the distance over towards Mareuil and Sartrouville. Along the slope the children went to work without a word, busy as squirrels gathering nuts for the winter. In a couple of minutes every single potato which had fallen on the road had been heaped below the gipsies' encampment.

Cady went at it like a bull at a gate, anxious to do his best to pay the Rouviers for his board and lodging. A whole sack had fallen on the verge without splitting. Here was a hundredweight at one stroke! He caught two of the corners and began tugging it towards him, and then to heave it along the rough track.

'Drop that sack at once!' a voice above him called.

He stopped short and looked up. On top of the bank two threatening shapes emerged slowly from the fog, slipping on the damp turf. These were real scrap-merchants. Cady recognised the breed, burly thugs who night after night break into stores and building-sites, cosh the night-watchmen and make off with cables, girders and piping.

One was tall and one was short, but both were un-shaven and both wore oil-stained donkey-jackets and thick fur-lined boots. The tall one had a green felt hat pulled down over his eyes. His nightmare face with its broken nose and scarred cheeks split into a horrid grin.

'You hear me? Drop that sack and get to hell out of it!' he shouted harshly.

Both strode forward, swinging their fists. Cady showed them his teeth. He clung to his find, determined not to give it up without a fight.

'Come and get it,' he said cheekily.

35

His snigger halted the two men a few yards short.

'You dirty little thief!' the big one exclaimed. 'I'll smash every bone in your body and from here to the Porte de Clichy they'll hear you crying for your mummy.'

'Haven't got one,' Cady retorted. 'But if I did yell, you wouldn't last a round with the crowd that would come running.'

By now he could sense them massing in silence at the end of the road. Hastily boys and girls alike had snatched up sticks and stones, closed their ranks and then come loping up to the cross-roads.

'Thieves yourselves,' Cady heard Sandra's calm retort from just behind him. 'You're yellow! Just you touch that sack! There's twenty-six of us, including our mate, and the gipsies are among them. From here to the bank it's our land. You put one foot on it and you'll have us all on top of you at once, just like you did in the Casbah. If anyone does start yelling, it'll be the weaker of you two, to your fat friend Théo, for help. But by the time he and his soaks get here we'll have smashed you to pulp.'

Beside her, Zalko and the Boubarka brothers chuckled and undid their brass-buckled belts. The two men made a show of lighting their cigarettes and then made off with a wary eye on the silent crowd which seemed as though it were gathering itself to spring. At last their figures disappeared into the fog and Cady let go of his sack with a sigh of relief.

'You've just met Monsieur Horace—the Mangler,' Sandra told him. 'He was the big one in the green hat. He'll pinch anything that's going, even the stray potatoes tumbling into our saucepans.'

'Who was the little bloke?'

'His second-in-command, Felletin Désiré. We call him Felletin the Cosh, because he's always got one up his sleeve to silence anyone who answers him back. The other twelve or so of them are just as bad. There you are, that rotten mob runs Bois-Bréau with a reign of terror. During the day all the men are on the Plastorex or some other building-site, doing the dirty work. Their wives are kept busy enough with the cooking and the washing at home. As you can guess the Mangler's lads have a clear run, and if anyone gets into their bad books, they simply wreck his shack. The only couple who could stand up to them are the Good Samaritan from the Green House and his girl-friend with the long nose. But those two look as though they'd blow away in a puff of wind and you can't see them lasting long against those yobs. So that leaves us kids. The trouble is we're so divided. Most of us stick to our little patch, like the Portuguese and the gipsies, and only leave it to go out and fight the gang next door. Now I'm pretty sure that if only we got together we could smash the Mangler's mob and fix him really good. It wouldn't be any riskier than the way we fight each other now—and it would be a lot more fun. We ought to think this one out . . . '

Cady shook his head.

'You don't know the enemy well enough to bring him down the proper way.'

'What do you mean?'

'The Mangler's weak spot isn't here in Bois-Bréau. Our best move would be to try to catch him where he isn't expecting us. Say in his own scrap-yard.'

His remark astonished Sandra, for it showed that Cady was as cunning as he was bold.

'We'll have a quiet word about that together some other time,' she muttered.

The gipsies had allowed them to stack the potatoes by their encampment in an overgrown hollow which hid the heap completely both from the shanty-town and from the cross-roads. They guarded the loot for a little while and did not lay a finger on it until the others had collected bags, boxes and even the baby's pram. Then Zalko divided it fairly and each hastily removed his share. Cady, who had not given an inch when the two toughs loomed out of the fog, was awarded the whole sack and bore it off in triumph, helped by Simbad and César Mahmadou.

Madame Meunier and Monsieur Langelin stood outside the Green House and watched the robber band come staggering back beneath their precious burdens.

'Like some?' Mimile offered, as he showed them the splendid smooth-skinned potatoes.

They blushed and declined his offer.

'I hope they taste good,' was all their Guardian Angel said.

'They're bound to taste better than old Bofano's,' Simbad retorted.

'And how did the accident happen?' Madame Meunier asked reproachfully.

César Mahmadou pointed innocently to the soft grey sea which welled over the shanty town.

'It was the fog, miss, just the fog. It's always the same. You hear something like a thunder-clap from the Croix-Souci cross-roads and then you find the roadway covered with all sorts of things.'

'What did you think?' an indignant Sandra added. 'We aren't wreckers, you know! The fuzz ought to be on duty at the cross-roads, but they're never there when they're needed. If people are in all that hurry, they should watch out. Anyway, the insurance company pays for the damage and the cargo, everybody knows that.'

Pimpin Léonard had been unable to finish the crazy story he had begun to tell his attentive friends. He set his two full baskets at Monsieur Langelin's feet and stared him boldly in the face.

'I really and truly believe in your story of the loaves

38

and the fishes,' he declared with conviction. 'But, if you ask me, it must have happened the same way as those Belgian spuds just done. There was César Mahmadou in the place of your Jesus. Over went a lorry and he tells his mates right away. Everyone goes rushing off to the cross-roads, and there you are!'

The despised apostle of the shanty-towns dared not utter a word. He watched the innocents go on their way, laden with enough food to last them till the other side of Christmas. Monsieur Langelin could well believe that Pimpin Léonard, in his innocence, had come very near the truth, in attributing to luck, bad weather, and a sharp-eyed watcher, the miracle which the hungry awaited.

Madame Meunier was thoughtful as her long nose quivered towards the Champs-Elysées of Bois-Bréau.

'Cady's here,' she said rapturously. 'His dirty little hands can heal anything, but something tells me he's got other tricks up his sleeve.'

3

Growing Teeth

AFTER THE depressing grey fogs of the past week, at last
they had a clear and golden morning, when there was not
a cloud in the pale blue sky. The sun shone and Cady
could now gaze at a world which he had only glimpsed in
snatches on the days before. Away to the north you could
see the rolling mass of russet and dark green which was
the Forest of Saint-Germain, while, towards Paris, rose
what looked like the battlements of a huge wall running
from Rueil to Saint-Denis; rows of factory buildings with
their saw-tooth roofs, their towering hoists, and their
gigantic chimneys crowned by plumes of smoke which the
wind slowly drove across the city.

Ever since their raid upon the potatoes, Sandra had
been venturing each evening at about the same time into
the least healthy parts of Bois-Bréau. Her sole companion
was the one and only dog in the village, Pignouf, a
muddy-looking mongrel, who belonged to nobody and
who scavenged for his food among the filth beside the
Wadi Radam.

Tackling the hardest first, she had begun by winning
over a dozen young Portuguese, after long and exhausting
argument. The gipsies, too, needed a lot of persuading.
Some feared to lose their independence, while the more
cunning did not look forward to an alliance with this big,
tough, brown-haired girl who planned to start a war on
the other side of the road, right on their doorstep as it
were.

'Up to now,' Zalko argued, 'we've lived nice and quiet in our caravans. The Mangler's men haven't bothered us, so why should we go out of our way to bring them down on us?'

'They're scared of what you'd do to them.' Sandra laughed. 'Your dads get their money from some pretty shady deals, so there's not much to choose between them as far as that's concerned. They'll touch their hats to one another across the road and go down to Théo's to have a drink together, but you can count on one thing for sure—once the Mangler finds you in his way, his strong-arm men will get rid of you like *that*.'

'How can we get in his way?'

'It's quite simple. By the end of next year, the Plastorex trading-estate will reach the road. Demagny's Warehouses will be bought up and pulled down and then the demolition boys will get busy on your dear old neighbours. The obvious thing the Scrap-metal King will do is to move over the road and in with us—after he's sent four or five bulldozers through the place. And you'll be the first to suffer, don't forget.'

The Gomez and the Bauers were deeply impressed by what she told them. All the same, their leader shrugged.

'It won't take us long to hitch up our sleeping-cars. The whole bunch of us can just go and find somewhere else to settle.'

'You'll be sorry to go,' Sandra murmured. 'It's a good spot, and apart from the Mangler, there isn't a cloud in your sky.'

The sharpest of the lot was Lucien Bauer. He leaned towards Sandra and chuckled.

'We'd like to come in with you, but how do you reckon to get rid of the Mangler and his mob? Blast them out with a field-gun, or with sticks of dynamite?'

'Something a lot better than that. You've enough

brains in your head to know that there's not much point in digging for copper or nickel round Paris, because there isn't any. So how does the Mangler manage to turn the stuff out of his foundry in the shape of bars and ingots which he can sell at a high old price to people who don't ask any questions?'

'Everybody knows that one,' Loulou Gomez sniggered. 'When the moon's right, old Green Hat and his mob go hunting two or three times a week, and every time they come home, there's a good heavy load under the tarpaulins on their truck. The gang gets its raw materials from source—some warehouse with either an old-age pensioner as nightwatchman, or no nightwatchman at all. They're a ruthless bunch, but they're careful and they get the tip-offs.'

Sandra readily agreed, and then she went on, 'The more they do it the more chance there is that one of these nights they'll come unstuck and collect about thirty years inside between them. If that happened, why, mates, we'd have got them off our backs for good and all.'

Despite her enthusiasm, the others were hesitant and doubtful.

'They haven't let any of us into their secrets,' Zalko retorted sarcastically. 'If you could change yourself into a puff of wind, that would be fine. Every now and then you could breeze in behind the old Mangler's armchair and come back and tell us what he and his lads were up to. Can you think of any other way of finding out?'

'Maybe I could. Suppose we got him into some scheme we'd made up by ourselves. We talk about it under the windows of the "Eldorado". Théo tells his mates about it and before you know what, the boss has been tipped off. If he takes the bait, then we've got him cold.'

It was no more than a suggestion made on the spur of the moment, but it was enough to persuade the gipsies to

come in on her side. First and foremost they had to collect
every bit of information they could about the daily routine
of the scrap-yard, watch the comings and goings of the
lorries, and learn to spot the tiny signs which revealed that
they were getting ready in the yard for yet another raid.

From that moment the fighting and feuding in the
shanty-town stopped. The fringe of bushes along the road
was split into three zones of observation with a team of
look-outs permanently on watch.

That morning Cady was working the Franco-Italian
part of the shanty-town with the twins, Violet and Rosie.
This sharp little pair were giving him a running com-
mentary on the bunch of crooks assembled by Monsieur
Kovacovici, commonly known as the Mangler.

'You've met the boss himself,' Violet was saying, 'and
Felletin the Cosh. You've only to take one look at them to
know they've got lumps of stone where their hearts ought
to be. Besides them, there's Big Jules, who runs the
scrap-yard for them. You don't see him much in the
village, but you've only to hang around outside the yard
for five minutes before he sticks his ugly snout through
the gate. Fat Théo keeps an eye on the shanty-town, and
he's got his strong-arm men, Spud and Battling Flagada,
to come out of the canteen when he tells them and lay into
anyone who's slow about paying. If the town of Bois-
Bréau gave a prize for the ugliest, dirtiest inhabitant, that
horrible trio would win it every time. Sometimes, when
they've bitten off more than they can chew, the Mangler
sends his yobs down to help them out. There's Old
Fred—he's white-haired, but don't go by that—King
Kong, a hairy brute, big Bouboule, who breaks down
doors by leaning on them, and the Crocodile. He's tall and
thin, he never says a word or seems to care about
anything, but he's the worst of the lot.'

'And here's a word of warning,' Rosie added. 'If ever you see that mob coming down the Champs-Elysées, just you beat it across the Wadi Radam. Some of the Algerians are always out of work and as they're pretty good at defending themselves, the Mangler's men don't dare to come that way.'

Cady had been keeping a count on his fingers as they listed these sinister figures.

'Any more?'

'We don't know so much about them,' Violet went on. 'First of all there are the drivers—Dormouse, he always seems asleep, even when he's driving, and Filochard, the car-thief, he's a smart one. Then you've got the labourers who work the hydraulic press, Marius and Bébé-Cadum, a couple of toughs you wouldn't touch with a barge-pole. Last of all there are the foundry workers, Arsène and Philippon, and they hardly ever stir outside their shop. I think that's the lot. Of course, we've never seen a skirt behind the Mangler's fence. No woman would want to live in a crowd like that. Hang on! Here comes the Dormouse and he's heading for Mareuil. Doesn't he look as though he's fast asleep when he's driving?'

'Has the Mangler only one lorry?' Cady asked.

'Two. The other's an old red Ford with a winch at the back. They usually bring that out at nights, to go and pinch stuff off the building-sites.'

Cady watched the Berliet vanish round the corner and then turned to stare at the endless wall which blocked the skyline on the other side of the road. Demagny's Warehouses. The words were painted in eye-stopping red, well-spaced and almost the height of the wall itself. Between the word *Demagny's* and the word *Warehouses* stood an enormous gateway, each post advertising the firm's activities, in smaller letters, *Repository, Storage, Delivery and Forwarding Agents*.

By contrast with the hustle and bustle on the Plastorex site, a strange silence reigned over this fortress, only occasionally disturbed by the arrival or departure of a furniture van. Then there would be a dull rumble as the great gates swung open to give a glimpse of two gloomy lines of buildings on either side of yards so vast it was impossible to see where they ended.

'That's pretty well guarded,' Violet observed.

'With neighbours like that, it would need to be,' Cady retorted. 'Have they ever fallen out?'

'Never. Some days the Mangler lets the warehouse people borrow his drivers and workmen.'

'How do you know?'

'Every now and then we see the Dormouse or Filochard coming in at the wheel of a different lorry. Generally Old Fred and the others are right behind them to give the storemen a hand.'

Suddenly there was a piercing whistle and young Beppo came running up the slope with his little sister Serafina close behind.

'Come quick! Théo and his thugs are at our place. We must do something . . . '

Cady and his companions raced to the corner of the alley. The Torrentes' shack, one of the best-built in Bois-Bréau, stood on the main street, not far from Bofano's grocery. The bartender's deep voice and Madame Torrente's shrill cries had drawn some fifty onlookers to the scene of the argument. These were mainly women in their aprons, some with a baby in the crook of their arm. The women just watched and listened, without making the slightest move to interfere. At Bois-Bréau you were far too scared of what might happen to you to take sides in a row of this kind. It was every man for himself and the Mangler take the hindermost!

'Three hundred francs! If I don't get it now, your shack comes down!' Fat Théo roared.

Dark-haired little Madame Torrente defended her patch of earth with furious energy.

'My husband gave you a hundred francs the day before yesterday! You promised to leave us in peace for the rest of the year!'

'Torrente only cleared a quarter of his arrears. I want the rest now!'

'Come back tonight! We'll have time to straighten things out. He can ask for an advance of wages.'

'I'm not waiting until tonight, I want it now! I let your place to four Spanish labourers yesterday. Pay me cash and I'll fix them up somewhere else. Otherwise—out you go!'

'I haven't fifty francs in my purse, even! Give me an hour or so . . . '

'Five minutes, time for you to clear your junk out! Come on, you lot, get busy!'

Grinning and flexing their muscles, Spud and Battling Flagada in their oil-stained overalls encircled the shack with a steel cable equipped with a ring at one end. The onlookers closed in to watch them. They knew the procedure at these scenes which filled the shanty-town with the atmosphere of a battlefield each time they occurred.

Madame Torrente went for the bartender with her claws out, but one backhander from him and she was sprawling on the ground. Meanwhile Beppo had run round the shack to get at the other two. A smack on the head sent him staggering. Cady tried to rush to his assistance, but the twins clung one to each arm and held him back.

'Stay where you are. You'll never beat them. If you go for those thugs, they'll beat you to death and then take it out on the Rouviers for your interference.'

46

Spud and Battling Flagada met once more in front of the shack and hauled on the cable, tightening it round the flimsy wooden walls. Madame Torrente and her children rushed inside and all three hurriedly removed bedding, chairs, table and the rest of their odds and ends which came flying out of the door and the window. Suddenly the crowd turned to the end of the main street down which came the rumble of a lorry. The Mangler's old red Ford bumped down the muddy track, a grinning young mechanic at the wheel.

'Filochard!' Violet told Cady. 'You can't beat him when it comes to knocking down shacks in Bois-Bréau. Not even a concrete-pillbox could stand up to his truck. Now you'll see some fun!'

The crowd drew back to give him room to manoeuvre. Beppo and Serafina clung to their mother's arms and tried to pull her away, but Madame Torrente stayed to pick up the last remaining bundles. To the amusement of the demolition men, as she went, she shouted:

'You wait till tonight! My husband and his mates'll pay you back for this. I'll promise, you won't do a thing like this again!'

The red lorry swung round and backed up against the front of the shack. Théo, who had been holding the hook, dropped it smartly into the ring of the winch-cable. A couple of turns drew it taut and there was a grinding noise as its hold tightened. Filochard engaged the gears and gradually revved the engine so that its noise drowned the yells and whistles of the crowd. There was a horrible crack and the walls of the shack came apart, were torn from their foundations and dragged into the middle of the main street like a bundle of fire-wood.

Cady heard a shout from the opposite direction and looked round. Sandra and a gang of their friends were coming down the street armed with stones and stout

47

sticks. Their first volley shattered the windscreen of the red lorry. The driver panicked, jammed his foot on the accelerator and shot off down the track. Théo and his strong-arm men had just unfastened the cable and now they were suddenly faced by a yelling mob. The hate that glittered in every eye made them lose their nerve.

'So you want a fight, do you?' Sandra screamed at them. 'Well, you'll get one. To start with, from now on nobody's going to pay you another penny in rent.'

The three men struck out blindly to escape the crowd and take refuge in the canteen. As he slammed the door, Théo turned.

'I'll tell the boss to cut off the water!' he shouted at the enraged mob. 'At both ends of the village, too, and right away!'

'And we'll cut off your wine!' Simbad retorted. 'The water doesn't belong to you, it comes from a public reservoir. If the Mangler lays his little finger on one of the water-pipes, your shack'll go up in flames an hour after!'

To back this threat a volley of stones broke every window in the canteen. Sandra had a job to cool the excitement and silence the wild talk of burning down the 'Eldorado' then and there.

'That's enough for the time being. You see what we can do once we get together? If César had only told me ten minutes before, the Torrentes' place would still be standing.

'Now we want a few of us to keep one eye on that end of the road—I expect Filochard'll come back any minute now with reinforcements. Leaving the nippers out of it, there's a good fifty of us. If we all stand firm, we can deal with the brutes.'

Somewhat unwillingly the crowd of onlookers began to scatter, muttering disagreeably among themselves.

'You rotten cowards!' Sandra yelled after them. 'You're

yellow! You're no better than the crooks who rook you of a quarter of your wages so that you can live in pigsties!'

'You won't change a thing!' an old harridan retorted. 'You aren't the first to try, and they were men, real men, tough men. The Mangler fixed them all right. Got their firms to sack them. When old Rouvier comes home with his cards, you'll know the reason why.'

Madame Torrente stood like a figure of stone in the midst of her scattered belongings with the tears streaming down her face. Cady and the twins collected the pots and pans lying strewn in the mud. Some way off, Beppo and Serafina were picking up the scattered planks, the sheets of corrugated iron, the panels of plaster-board and ply-wood which had sheltered them from the wind and the rain.

'We'll help you get this lot sorted out,' Sandra told the little Italian woman. 'You own the land and the planks as well. Théo's made you pay ten times what they're worth, so you don't owe him a penny-piece. Your husband was quite right to stand up to him. If everyone got together and did the same we'd soon get rid of that rotten mob. When Monsieur Torrente comes back from work tonight he and his mates'll soon have the wall up and the corrugated iron on the roof. You'll sleep in your own home tonight and I promise you that nobody's going to upset you again.'

The Algerians and the gipsies had been keeping a sharp lookout from the edge of the shanty-town, but the Mangler had not condescended to show his face. The watchers had noticed no suspicious movements from behind the fence round the scrap-yard.

'They must have something else on their plate,' Zalko said. 'Probably to do with the police, or their rivals over in Sartrouville or Epinay. Once they've settled whatever it is, they'll be back in the red truck to rescue Théo and his couple of merry men. If we don't watch out, they'll knock half the village down.'

Simbad grinned wolfishly.

'That old lorry of theirs won't get twenty yards down the street,' he said confidently. 'In the first place we'll all be there, even after dark: and in the second place, they're scared of something. It came over them the other day, when they were fighting for that sack of spuds with us.'

'Scared of what?' Lucien Bauer asked. 'Sandra and her dozen kids wouldn't frighten metal-thieves like them.'

'The first person the Mangler and the Cosh met,' said Simbad, 'when they came down the bank, was the stranger, the kid with the brand-new boots. Where's Cady sprung from? Search me. But they looked a bit rum when they caught sight of him.'

'What's so special about him anyway?'

'Nothing, so far as we're concerned. But maybe the old Mangler doesn't like the way he laughs.'

By noon, the four walls of the Torrentes' shack were standing once more on their foundations, strengthened by whatever props came to hand. The furniture and fittings had been replaced with all the respect such a misfortune deserved. Then the boys and girls departed to get their dinner or their snack and returned to eat it in the sunshine, sitting in a row outside Bofano's grocery.

Opposite them, Théo and his thugs would occasionally venture their angry faces near the windows of the canteen, pulling them back at once as a stone-studded lump of mud came hurtling past. The siege went on until four in the afternoon. Every ten minutes a scout would be sent to the outposts, only to return with the same brief message, all quiet on the scrap-yard front. At night-fall, the strict watch was relaxed. Sandra relieved the sentries, sent the smaller children home, and, with only a handful of the bolder spirits beside her, kept a careful watch over the Torrentes' place.

The first person to poke his nose out of the canteen was Théo, and the stillness of the main street reassured him. From the corner of each alleyway ten pairs of eyes watched him as he puffed and panted his way up to the Green House. For the time being his power had vanished. Of course he would have to wait until knocking-off time, when the workers would come streaming into the bar of the 'Eldorado', to the casks of red wine which was drawn by the quart for these weary folk. Then it would be back to normal. The honest building workers from the Plastorex site would send their wives and children packing, and start drinking their pay away, unless . . .

'But that's the ticket,' Théo said to himself. 'One night off the booze will do them the world of good. My solid family men will think it's the end of the world, and as a result those wretched little window-smashers will get the biggest hiding of their lives.'

The Algerians brought him up with a start just opposite the chapel without a cross. The swarthy lads stirred in the twilight, gripping long pieces of timber studded with nails.

'Don't you touch the stopcock,' Simbad called. 'We know where it is. If the water dries up tonight, or tomorrow, or the day after that, we'll take you from your bed and give you a bubble-bath in the Wadi Radam. Don't you forget what I've said!'

Théo stared towards the road in desperation. The traffic was thinning out. There was no sign of help. Old Kovaco, as his gang called him among themselves, must be up to his neck in it and could not care less about his manor of Bois-Bréau.

It was growing darker and darker and patches of mist were rising from the Seine as on the previous evenings. As the bartender walked slowly back to the 'Eldorado', he became aware of furtive movements and muffled laughter, alternating with animal cries all around him. He had to admit that the Boss was right: in a shanty-town open to all comers, with its menfolk away all day, the kids were as destructive as rats. The problem was how to get rid of them.

The first labourers to come off the Plastorex site were met at the top of the track by a group of anxious women and by Sandra and some of the boys. Very briefly she explained about the eviction and the wild resistance offered to the wreckers.

Mad with rage, Monsieur Torrente and a group of Italians went straight down the road to find out just how much damage had been done. Meanwhile old Rouvier, whose opinions carried more weight than those of anyone else in the shanty-town, gave his grand-daughter an angry dressing-down.

'Have you gone completely mad? We shall have a fight on our hands again! The Mangler will make us pay for the windscreen in the Ford and the windows in the "Eldorado" by putting up our rents. It will be worse than ever when we're at work—his strong-arm men will come in and have a fine time smashing the place up, clearing people out of the best huts and putting old lags and loafers in their place to drive us to the other side of the wadi. A fine game you've been playing!'

'We aren't scared of those yobs,' Sandra answered calmly. 'The rats haven't dared show their faces so far. We've made up our minds that nobody's to pay Théo another penny. If we have to, we'll fight instead of you to defend our patch of land. Old Fred, the Crocodile and their mob will be overcome every time they try to attack. We'll show you . . . '

She signed to Beppo, who gave a shrill whistle. Within

seconds each neighbouring alleyway began to stir, and out of them poured a ragged army brandishing pokers and shovels, broomhandles, chunks of wood and sticks. This was the first time that all the children of the shanty-town had emerged from their lairs at the same time. They stood shoulder to shoulder at the top of the main street.

Old Rouvier gasped. 'I never knew there were so many of them.'

His workmates standing beside him stared in amazement. From the very beginning, neighbour had bickered with neighbour without a thought of the children growing up, never dreaming that they would one day be a new force, greedy for room to move and ready to fight anyone in their way.

Pimpin's father, Monsieur Léonard, turned to Bois-Bréau's oldest inhabitant.

'Your Sandrine's right. We've been fools to let these few yobs frighten us for so long. They've been getting worse and worse, because some of us were too scared to do anything and some of us didn't know what to do, and now as far as they're concerned, we're just a bunch of slobs who can't fight back and can be kicked into doing just what they want. And now you want our kids to stop trying to pay them back in their own coin? From now on I'm going to be like our mate Torrente—I'm not paying, not for the water, not for the site, not for anything!'

'Neither are we!' the rest of the group shouted back.

But Monsieur Rouvier remained unconvinced.

'You'll have forgotten all your fine resolutions by the time you go back to work tomorrow. Anyway the Mangler's a slippery customer. He'll insist on talking separately to the French, the Italians, the Spaniards, the Portuguese, the Algerians and the gipsies, and in the end the old rogue will have us all under his thumb again like he always does. And a fat lot of good all this will have done you.'

'We'll send him a spokesman or two who won't let him shout them down,' said Sandra.

'Young or old?'

'The sharpest in our gang, why not?'

Her grandfather roared with laughter.

'Ever seen the Mangler take any notice of kids?'

'Nobody's thought of trying to put him in his place,' Sandra went on. 'No, the boot's been on the other foot. And if we spot something fishy going on in the scrap-yard, we shan't be scared of shopping the Mangler.'

'I'm not having you mixed up in his racket, understand?' Monsieur Rouvier growled. 'You'd risk a lot more than a coshing. See?'

Sandra did not persist. She gave the order and her comrades scattered without a sound down the gloomy alleyways. On the crest of the rise the headlights of passing traffic caught more men as they crossed the road from the Plastorex site. In small groups they wound their way down the track to their respective parts of the shanty-town, discussing the latest news. One or two of them stopped outside the 'Eldorado' for some wine or a beer. With his chuckers-out on either side, Théo stood in the doorway to discourage any thought of a drink.

'No more wine and no more beer! I've shut the place until further notice. It's up to you to keep your kids in order.'

He pointed to the gaping windows and the walls spattered with filth, and gingerly felt the bruise on his nose which had got in the way of a missile. But the fat bartender's expectations were cruelly disappointed, for the fathers delayed the punishments which he had counted on their giving the children.

'We'll go over to Mareuil for a drink, then!' one of

54

them called to him. 'At least until Bofano can lay in a stock. It won't cost as much as yours, either, you old rogue!'

Beyond them there was a bustle of activity. The walls of the Torrentes' place were being strengthened, for a gust of wind in the night could have blown them over. But despite this cheerful demonstration of good-neighbourliness, Monsieur Rouvier was still out of temper when he got home, accompanied by Sandra, Mimile, Cady and the dog Pignouf, which sensibly stayed outside.

'We're building up to a disaster!' the old man told his wife. 'One of these nights Bois-Bréau's going to go up in flames like the shanty-town at Bobigny last winter. And what happened? A dozen or so burnt alive in their shacks, and another five hundred without a roof over their heads and the temperature ten below zero. The Mangler wouldn't care. He isn't scared by the size of the thing. You can cheat him and stand up to him to some extent without affecting the life of the place, but you can't fly in his face with sticks and stones like you did this morning, you silly little fools!'

He swung sharply round on Sandra.

'Who was the brainless dolt who put the idea into your head in the first place?'

'I did,' Cady said boldly, trying to avert the storm.

His sciatica forgotten, Monsieur Rouvier caught him by the ear and dragged him to the door.

'Out you go!'

Pignouf the faithful hound knew by the tone of voice that there would be no scraps for him, so he followed the boy as he walked away whistling. Taking great care as they crossed the Wadi Radam, both found shelter in the Boubarkas' smoky hovel.

'What's happened to the Rouviers?' Simbad asked in amazement.

55

'The old boy's got the jitters,' Cady answered. 'He's not sheltering a rebel under his cardboard roof. He's one of the people who are scared, and the Mangler and his scrap-merchants still mean something to them.'

'Didn't Sandra stick up for you?'

'I just beat it and left them my spuds. I wouldn't have wanted them to start throwing plates at each other 'cos of me.'

This made Monsieur and Madame Boubarka laugh. They crouched beside the stove on which stood a savoury-smelling saucepan.

'You can eat and sleep with us,' the sewage expert decided. 'But Pignouf must stay outside.'

'He's used to it,' Cady answered, speaking for them both.

4

The Grey Lorry

A FEW days later the Guardian Angel of Bois-Bréau departed from his usual routine and turned up at the Green House at about eight in the morning, well before Madame Meunier. Much to his surprise, he saw two tousled figures huddled up against one another on the camp-bed in the surgery. Pignouf was the first to open one eye, but he shut it again almost at once with a sigh of contentment.

Cady awoke more slowly and it was the smell of fresh coffee wafting round the room which brought him to. He struggled up on one elbow and respectfully accepted the cup offered to him.

'Weren't you all right with the Boubarkas?' Monsieur Langelin asked him severely.

'I was okay, but I didn't want to scrounge off them. Anyway, last evening the Torrentes asked me if I'd like to come to them. I thought I'd better say no. They're even worse off and they've just been through a sticky patch.'

'What about the Rouviers?'

'I'm just waiting for the old man to get another go of sciatica; I shan't have to wait long with the cold weather coming on. Meantime, Sandra keeps me going with what she can nick from their larder.'

'In other words,' said an unsmiling Monsieur Langelin, 'you thought it would be handier if you came sneaking into the welfare centre with that old flea-bag . . . '

Pignouf did not protest.

'How did you get in, through the door or through the window?'

'Through the door,' Cady replied. 'With a duplicate key Zalko gave me.'

The Guardian Angel's eyebrows rose and his pale face flushed slightly.

'A duplicate key? So the gipsies come wandering in whenever they please?'

'Only the three oldest women in the tribe, and they always come at night. Anyway they've never pinched a thing off you, even when you've left a box full of stuff.'

An astonished Monsieur Langelin agreed that this was so.

'Well, whatever can they be up to then, in a hole like this, in the middle of the night?'

'Nothing. The three old witches think you've got God hidden somewhere on the premises. They light a little oil lamp at the end of the room, sit down and watch it burning in silence. That satisfies them. Then they cross themselves and go back to their camp.'

Monsieur Langelin lowered his head to hide his embarrassment. He took a few sips of coffee, brought a ham sandwich out of his haversack and divided it between himself and Cady. Both ate in silence, but they did not forget the dog and Pignouf's jaws snapped loudly round the occasional scrap. Then, having drunk what was left of the coffee, the Guardian Angel turned to his visitor.

'I'm told you haven't let the grass grow under your feet at Bois-Bréau.'

Cady guessed at once what he meant.

'Yes, people are beginning to get to know me. I go my rounds when the men get back from work in the evenings. The Portuguese are the most suspicious. Even when you've cured them properly, they mutter something about witchcraft. It's not true. It's just a matter of

58

being able to manipulate bones and muscles strained by overwork.'

'That all?'

Cady held out a pair of rather grubby hands.

'They've never hurt a soul. Some people have told me that my hands give out an intense heat when I'm treating them. But that's something I can't control. Old Augustine had the same thing.'

He smiled for a moment to himself, and then went on.

'It all helps us kids. The healer acts as a sort of link man. Since I've been doing my home treatments the different parts of the village have been getting on together much better.'

The Guardian Angel nodded and then displayed a touch of anxiety.

'Any news of the thugs?'

'Apart from their normal business they haven't stirred outside their yard. There was a bit of a commotion, though, yesterday morning. Filochard came down on his own in the red lorry to deliver four casks of beer to the canteen. Before you could say knife we'd got the whole gang ready in front of Bofano's place. Nobody said a word, and we were all ready for a real scrap, but he was away like the wind. Théo's put back the broken glass and opened the bar again, but only about a dozen use the place now. Spud and Battling Flagada try to pretend we aren't there. All in all, the family have stood firm and nobody pays a penny of rent now.'

'Watch it, all the same. The Mangler's cooking up one of his usual ploys. When all his gang come marching down the street, you'll be knocked head over heels to the other side of the Wadi Radam.'

'I know that all right,' Cady admitted. 'And really all we can do is wait and watch from the edge of the shanty-town. But it isn't us they're scared of.'

'Who, then?'

'I've got the feeling someone else is keeping an eye on them on the quiet. So they've got to lie low because a pitched battle would bring the spotlight on them.'

'The police?'

'Could be. And it isn't here they're being watched, either.'

'The Mangler's a thorough-paced villain, we're all agreed, but he's very careful about the way he runs things. You're not going to catch him in the act . . . '

'You're wrong there,' Cady laughed. 'The scrap-metal trade is just a front for the Mangler and his gang.'

Monsieur Langelin stared at him in bewilderment.

'Is this just one of your guesses?'

'No, I'm sure of it.'

'How did you find out?'

Cady raised his right leg and then his left.

'All through a pair of boots.'

Monsieur Langelin stared at them and frowned.

'What's so special about them?'

'Apart from the fact that they're comfortable, nothing as far as I'm concerned. All the same, interfering busy-bodies might very much like to know where they came from.'

'And where did they come from?'

'Ali Baba's Cave—it isn't far away.'

But Cady did not give its exact geographical position and changed the subject rather abruptly.

'In her day, Old Augustine used to be able to cure anybody with her magical hands, even of the pain of a malignant tumour. She wasn't a bad teacher either, and she could take a broad view of world affairs. "If you ask me," she used to say, "all these disasters hang on a straw. People laugh at anyone with the sense to warn them before it happens. Who can worry about a straw?" Now although I haven't checked it myself, all hope is not yet lost.'

60

'What did she mean by disaster?' Monsieur Langelin asked. 'Had she our little community of Bois-Bréau in mind?'

'No, only the Scrap-metal King and his shady deals.'

Then Cady bent down to pat his new boots with satisfaction. At the top of the leg each bore a little white trade mark stamped into the rubber—a vulture with wings outspread.

There was a long silence. To hide his unease, the Guardian Angel began to pace the room. Buried in the boy's talk was a resolve, he felt, which took him far away from his humble task.

Cady stood beside him in the open doorway. First they sent the dog out and then they looked outside as warily as two hunters in ambush. By now the men had scattered among the tangle of building operations on the site across the road, but the shanty-town lay quiet and slumbering and the chill of the morning still cut the body.

'I hope I'll see you again soon,' Monsieur Langelin said shyly. 'Bring Sandra and the others. There'll be hot milk and bread and butter for everyone, Madame Meunier's promised me. After the toddlers have had their lesson, there'll be a sing-song to cheer everyone up and then I'll go on with my stories. The weather's getting bad and they'll be all the more appropriate.'

'Christmas is in the air,' Cady admitted.

He tried to go, but the Guardian Angel held his arm.

'This horrible dump is no place for you,' he said, his other arm gesturing towards the shanty-town spread out before them. 'Do you like it so much in Bois-Bréau?'

'I haven't finished learning to live yet,' the boy sighed as he gently freed himself.

The words pierced Monsieur Langelin through and through.

'I expect you're right.' His voice was low. 'Nowadays

the only high adventure left for those the world has
forgotten is to haul themselves out of their poverty by
their own efforts.'

Wasting an hour or two in the Green House over
Madame Meunier's bread and butter was out of the
question now that Théo and his two bouncers had begun
to stalk the alleyways once more. Cady did not even pass
the invitation on to Sandra—she would have turned it
down, anyway. He therefore took his turn on watch with
the twins just above the part of the village where the
Italians lived.

There was nothing to report from Demagny's Warehouses. The great gates stayed shut all morning. Beyond
him the gipsies reported some activity and the shifting of
stocks behind the fence round Kovacovici & Co. However,
the hydraulic press remained idle and no smoke rose from
the foundry chimney.

Violet and Rose took their friend back to dinner with
Madame Belin. She was a gentle soul who tended the only
pot-plant in the shanty-town, a geranium which stood
beside her door. The afternoon glided by just as peacefully, but with extra vigilance on the children's part. The
Mangler generally timed his reprisal raids for the hours of
dusk, and each stood to his post and strained his eyes.

The Portuguese and the Spaniards, whom Sandra had
had such difficulty in persuading to join in, had chosen an
olive-skinned boy called Manoel Pereira as their leader.
Although he seemed a weedy specimen, the orders he gave
in a hissing voice were rigidly obeyed. Most of them had
shown their mettle during the bombardment of the
canteen, and from then on they had been given as their
observation-post the thicket flanking the gipsies' encampment, a few yards from the Croix-Souci cross-roads.

It was after half past five, and the lights along the main

road had just come on, when one of the lads on watch came sliding down the bank to join the bulk of the gang assembled in the sunken road. At last he had something worth reporting.

'A lorry's just broken down a couple of hundred yards away, this side of the railway bridge.'

'One of the Mangler's lorries?' Manoel asked.

'No,' the little look-out, Pepe Garcia, replied. 'It's a big grey lorry, a twenty- or thirty-tonner. Doesn't look to have a name on it, and it seems brand-new.'

'How do you know it's broken down?'

'The driver got out of the cab and fiddled about under the bonnet. Then he tried his self-starter a dozen or more times. It wouldn't work. So he stuck his red warning triangle in the road, and walked off towards the cross-roads.'

'Was the lorry loaded or empty?'

'Don't know. It's got a big metal body and it's shut at the back. But it's riding too high to be fully loaded.'

'Off you go as fast as you can and let that French girl know. Tell her we're waiting for her here.'

Leaving a few of the bigger boys on guard in the alley by the Torrentes' shack, Sandra came running at once with Simbad, César Mahmadou and Cady, and Cady's inseparable companion Pignouf.

'Let's have a closer look at it,' she said to Manoel. 'But don't go all together, we don't want to attract attention.'

Manoel took with him Gil Torres, his second-in-command, and the little Spanish look-out, who did not want to miss the fun. Once past the Croix-Souci cross-roads, the gang prudently crept through the wastelands beside the road.

'Here comes the driver!' Pepe whispered.

The man was striding along the left-hand verge. He

never noticed them as they passed, but at that very moment a car came towards him and his face was illuminated by the headlights.

'But that's the Dormouse!' Sandra exclaimed. 'Your broken-down lorry is only the Mangler's Berliet.'

'Oh no it isn't!' Pepe protested. 'I'm not making it up. My lorry's a Willème. It's a grey one, and I've never seen it in the scrap-yard before.'

They looked back to the cross-roads. The Dormouse continued down the Mareuil road and went in through the yard gate.

'I expect he's gone to get someone to tow him in,' said César Mahmadou. 'Get a move on, we want to have a look before he comes back.'

The mysterious lorry had stopped not far from the bridge, as Pepe had said, with its side-lights on and the warning sign standing at the regulation distance on a road already damp with mist. The Dormouse had left the nearside door to the cab wide open.

'He must have been in a tearing hurry,' Manoel muttered.

There was nobody in the cab, so Sandra climbed nimbly up and peered inside by the dim blue light of the dashboard. There were a few papers scattered on the seat and a black oilskin coat hanging by the other door, and that was all. Above her, the recess containing the bunk was half hidden by a curtain. She scrambled down and shook her head.

'The Mangler's new toy, I expect.'

'Why don't we try to get in at the back?' Simbad asked her.

'Go ahead, but make it snappy. The Dormouse could be back any minute now.'

Three of them had to get together to unfasten the massive doors at the back and open them an inch or two.

Simbad switched on his torch and shone it into the opening.

'Not a sausage,' he said a moment later, disappointed. 'Not even a pound of potatoes.'

His remark made the two Portuguese laugh. They had heard about that windfall business. Cady, however, had stayed on the verge, beside the open door. He stared up into the cab with eager curiosity. To get a better view he climbed inside and lowered himself into the padded seat. His movement set off a strange whirring noise in the bunk above him and a guttural voice addressed him from behind.

'Well, me old fruit, aren't you going to say hullo to Igor?'

Rigid with shock, the boy did not dare move as he anxiously wondered what would happen next. Sandra and the dog came running to the door.

'Who was that?'

'Not me,' Cady stuttered. 'There was someone in the bunk.'

'You're seeing things! I looked a moment ago and there was nobody there!'

She looked up and suddenly burst out laughing. There, perched on the edge of the bunk, a black bird with a red beak was watching them with glittering eyes.

'Well,' he said in the same grumpy voice, 'aren't you going to say hullo to Igor?'

Now that Cady had got over the shock he was greatly relieved to be able to remember his manners.

'Hullo, Igor, how are you?'

'Not so bad, and you?' the bird answered pat.

He added, so coolly that it left them gasping, 'You buying a drink, or are we going straight on?'

Thinking to exhaust his repertoire, Cady willingly continued, 'I don't mind . . . what will you have?'

65

'The usual. A stiff Pernod for Igor, and a beer for the boys.'

'And then?'

'Charlie will take the wheel,' the bird went on, without losing the thread of the conversation, 'and off we head to Lyons. First stop just outside Paris at Mother Dutilleul's. Then change drivers at two in the morning. Don't worry, I'll wake old Gaston. Jump to it, lads! Put your foot down and keep your eyes open, I don't want to finish the night in the ditch!'

He ended his speech with a prolonged whistle, and then stretched his neck out as if he expected the conversation to continue. Their cosy chat was interrupted by César Mahmadou calling anxiously:

'Beat it, quick! The red lorry's just come out of the scrap-yard and it's heading for the bridge.'

Cady jumped down and followed his friends into the darkness of the wastelands. At first they hid behind a broken-down wall to watch the lorry-repairers at work. All the skill and knowledge of Filochard and the Dormouse was powerless to bring the grey lorry's engine to life once more and in the end they had to take it in tow. Once they had turned her right round—a manoeuvre which took them right off the road at one point—the smaller vehicle took the larger in tow, and made off for the cross-roads like a red ant dragging the corpse of some large beetle behind it.

'Where are they taking it?' Sandra asked. 'You got a clue?'

'Back to Demagny's Warehouses, I expect,' Cady promptly replied.

'Why there?'

'I was on watch with the Belin twins round there, that's my area, and I saw it come out of the warehouses and drive off towards the cross-roads.'

'When was this?'

'Under ten minutes ago. It's the very same lorry, I'm sure of that, because the Dormouse was driving it.'

'You might have told us a bit sooner.'

'I came down the road to do that, but young Pepe had just brought the news of the breakdown, so I thought you all knew anyway.'

They began to move closer and closer to the top of the bank as they watched the two lorries crawling at walking pace along the road below. When the vehicles reached the cross-roads they brought the traffic to a standstill.

'That's a rum sort of hare we've started!' Sandra exclaimed. 'Just think, if Filochard swung off to the right and took the whole lot into the scrap-yard!'

And that is precisely what happened a few minutes later, to everybody's utter surprise.

'The Mangler doesn't bother with empty lorries,' Simbad observed. 'Even if they're brand-new like this one.'

'Then why go to all this trouble?' Manoel retorted, picking his words carefully. 'The Dormouse could just as well have left her broken down by the bridge.'

Nobody could answer his question. Pignouf gave a throaty growl. For the last few seconds César Mahmadou had felt something fluttering round his fuzzy head like a huge butterfly. He swung his arms to drive it away, but whatever it was suddenly alighted on his shoulder and croaked in his ear:

'Well, me old fruit, aren't you going to say hullo to Igor?'

The poor African was scared out of his wits. He threw himself on the ground and buried his face in his arms. The bird immediately swapped perches and flapped over to Cady's shoulder. The twang of his voice had strongly impressed the others and the fog and the shifting light from the road increased the uncanny atmosphere. Simbad looked about him with staring eyes.

'I'm going crazy. . . . Did you all hear what I heard?'

Sandra showed him the odd-looking bird perched on Cady's shoulder.

'It was in the cab of the lorry. It's a black bird that talks like a parrot. Don't upset him, say hullo.'

'Hullo, Igor!' the Algerian obediently repeated.

'Hullo, old son!' the bird retorted. 'What about a little drop of something before we go? Then we load up and off. Six hundred miles from midnight to midday—Perpignan isn't next door, you know.'

As before, he ended by whistling loud and long, piercing Cady's eardrums. Cady suddenly had the bright idea of continuing the conversation by remembering what the bird had said before.

'Where's Charlie?'

The bird cocked its beak with almost a look of interest.

'Gone to have a drink with old Gaston at the bar on the corner.'

'What's your load tonight?'

'Ten tons of glass-ware for Rouen, and fifteen tons of jam for Le Havre. Look out, we don't want the whole ruddy lot in the ditch!'

Suddenly he took off from Cady's shoulder and vanished into the darkness, skimming like a partridge over the wastelands.

'You should have held his neck,' Sandra said with a touch of disappointment. 'Then we could have tied a bit of string to one of his legs and taken him back to Bois-Bréau.'

'Igor wouldn't have let you do it,' Cady answered gravely. 'He's somebody, you know.'

Still shaking, César Mahmadou stared round with frightened eyes.

'If he starts croaking in my ears again, I'll finish him off with a stick.'

'You think he'd make a good meal?' little Pepe asked, and they all shouted him down.

They set off again for the fog-dimmed lights of the cross-roads. Pepe's big brother Enrico was waiting for them at the bottom of the bank with his look-outs. All were very cold.

'Manage to scrounge anything?' he asked, his eyes alight with greed.

'The lorry was empty,' Manoel replied. 'All we found was a bird which talks nonsense and never stops asking for a drink. And anyway he's pushed off now ...'

Sandra had pity on their sufferings and sent them home at once. Then, as she and the others went on their way once more along the sunken road to the top of the village street, their little group was suddenly halted by a pair of wildly excited gipsies.

'It's the finest sight you ever saw in all your life!' Loulou Gomez exclaimed. 'They're fighting one another like mad in the scrap-yard!'

'It's as good as a ringside seat at Olympia!' Lucien Bauer added. 'Come on, follow us!'

Threading his way through the caravans with their glowing windows, he led them to the edge of the main road. Immediately opposite the encampment, the dilapidated fence round the scrap-yard rose and blocked the view, but a tiny corner of the yard could be seen through the bars of the gate. Shadowy figures were running in all directions, while others met in the half-light, trading blows and insults. In the background, the lighter mass of the two lorries, still joined by the tow-rope, stood out dimly against the soot-blackened sheds. Every now and then a shrill scream would come from the struggling mob

69

and the combatants would step back as a body fell to the ground.

There was a sharp hoot of a car horn and then headlights winked as the Mangler's long white Chevrolet came gliding over the cross-roads and braked outside the gate. The fight ceased abruptly. At once the rusty gates were opened to let the car in and then clanged mournfully shut upon the silent yard. The only sound was the muffled thunder of the traffic as it headed towards Paris.

'Just what's been going on?' Sandra asked.

Lucien Bauer took up the tale.

'We'd barely noticed the grey lorry driven past by the Dormouse, when ten minutes later, what did we see? Why there was that dozy idle individual hurrying back on foot! He never even asked Big Jules first, just opened up the gate and vanished into the background. I expect he was hunting up his pal Filochard. Soon after, they both came roaring out in the Ford. Out of the sheds came a dozen men led by Big Jules and the Crocodile, all waving their arms about. Then the mix-up started. Some of them wanted to shut the gates at once, while the others held on tight to keep them wide open. When the Ford came back towing that huge grey lorry, that really started things off and they began to hit out. The lorries had to force their way through and they nearly took the gates with them. Once they'd parked them outside the offices, Big Jules and his mates went for Filochard and the Dormouse, and the Crocodile and his lot waded in to help them. The Mangler got back just in time to stop murder being done . . . But can you understand what it's all about?'

'Not a clue!' Simbad laughed. 'What makes things even trickier is that the lorry came out of Demagny's Warehouses ten minutes before it all started.'

'Then why didn't they take it back there?'

'I expect because Green Hat and his boys are better equipped to repair it.'

'It looks to me as though the Mangler isn't at all happy the way things have gone,' Cady said. 'But one thing's for sure. That new lorry won't leave the yard unless it leaves in little pieces.'

Once more they stared at the still silent huddle of buildings. The lights in the office had now been switched on, as had the arc lamp over the gate, and they lit up the empty expanse of the yard. The two lorries had vanished, to be replaced by the Mangler's white Chevrolet. Seconds passed and then the red Ford bumped into view as it made its way round the workshops towards its garage.

At first glance anyone walking or driving through this grimy suburb would not have noticed anything out of the ordinary. You had to live on the spot, in close contact with these crooks who idled about the scrap-yard, to be aware that all this bustle was the prelude or the postscript to some criminal activity.

'They must have come unstuck somewhere,' was Simbad's view. 'At any rate we're okay for the time being. It doesn't look as though they're going to beat up Bois-Bréau tonight.'

'We'll keep a look-out on the gate until supper-time at least,' Zalko decided. 'If they start to stir again, Loulou can tip you off. Don't wander too far away.'

'We'll be at the top of the street,' Sandra assured him. 'There, or else behind the Green House, where the Africans hang out. The Mahmadous' tent collapsed this afternoon and César asked if we'd give a hand to put it up again.'

She went back to the village with her friends, the dog gambolling along behind them. Bois-Bréau's Champs-Elysées were lit by twenty dusty bulbs protected by iron mesh and hanging at irregular intervals from poles set drunkenly askew. Some of the shanties looked even more wretched and flimsy in these harsh pools of light which stretched like a necklace as far as the Wadi Radam. Beyond was the dark maze of the Casbah bounded by the walls and tall trees of Saint-Adrien's cemetery.

'Hullo, Théo's put on the street lights again,' César observed. 'That's the first time since we gave the canteen a pasting. What does that mean?'

'He's no fool, you know,' said Simbad. 'He's only turned it on while the men are coming back from work, so that he can lure them into his bar. After that he'll switch off again.'

The windows of the 'Eldorado' threw their light into the street and illuminated the grimy front of the grocery and the line of figures walking up and down outside, scarves wrapped round their heads and shopping baskets in hand.

'Shopping-time for the stony broke,' Sandra sighed. 'Bofano only gives tick now between five and seven at night, just to make the drinkers on the other side of the road feel bad. Monsieur Torrente and my grand-dad told him that's what he ought to do.'

As they emerged from the track, the black bird came swooping down like a dart, circled round them three times looking for somewhere comfortable to perch and in the end settled on Cady's shoulder.

'Hurrah!' shouted Simbad. 'It looks as though he's adopted you. I hope he's not too difficult to feed.'

'I'd rather do without him if you don't mind,' Cady protested. 'This wretched dog won't leave my heels as it is.'

'Buy us a drink, old fruit,' asked Igor in his ear.

'All that wretched crow can think about is booze,' an outraged César Mahmadou said.

The others shrieked with laughter.

'If I'd got any money,' Simbad said, 'I'd take him into Théo's and let him order a round. Old fat guts would fall over backwards.'

'And a stiff Pernod for Igor!' the bird croaked.

'There's some connection in what he says,' Cady admitted and gently lifted his hand.

At once Igor jumped from Cady's shoulder on to the pointed forefinger and held on tight with his yellow claws. His velvety black plumage was unrelieved except for a few spots of white and grey on the head. At some time in the past his wings had been clipped, but the flight feathers had begun to grow again unevenly, allowing him to fly for short distances with a characteristic whirring sound. His long red beak poked this way and that and his little black eyes, with white rims, stared from one face to the next with an expression of real intelligence.

'Shall we try to tie him up?' Simbad asked.

Sandra hesitated.

'What's the point? And anyway, if we do tie a piece of string to his leg, he might go on strike and stop talking. And that would be a shame.'

The sound of footsteps turned their attention away from the bird. It was Lucien Bauer coming down the track after them.

'Any news?' Sandra called to him.

'No, nothing to report. Zalko only wondered if one of you had taken the number of that lorry. It might come in handy.'

'I did think about that when I was opening up the back, but the number-plate was so covered with muck that you couldn't make out what it was.'

'Igor may know,' Sandra laughed.

Cady whistled softly between his teeth to attract the bird's attention.

'Come on, old son, tell us the number of your lorry.'

'9122 RB 06!' Igor shot back at him.

'There you are,' Sandra told the gipsy. 'It's as simple as that. Want a scrap of paper to jot it down?'

Slowly Lucien Bauer backed away, eyes as large as saucers; then he ran away to the camp as fast as his legs would carry him, pursued by the shrill laughter of the gang.

When the fun had died down, César Mahmadou said admiringly, 'That bird's a real devil!'

'I expect he knows all sorts of things we haven't begun to guess at yet,' Sandra said thoughtfully. 'I'd be quite prepared to take him home, but Grand-dad would have fifty fits if he heard Igor call him old fruit and keep ordering stiff Pernods . . . Will you look after him?'

She had turned to Cady who was carrying the bird on his wrist as gracefully as any falconer.

'If he's used to me,' he answered, 'I'd like to. But he and the dog will have to get on!'

'Where are you having your food tonight?'

'With the Portuguese. I've one or two patients to treat up there. Then I'll go back to my flat with Igor and Pignouf.'

And he pointed to the Green House standing cold and gloomy among the nearby hovels.

5

The Mangler's Blood Money

CADY WAS having a delightful dream. The Mangler's
fifteen villains, in long night-shirts and with ropes around
their necks, were walking down the track to Bois-Bréau to
make amends to the inhabitants clustered around their
Guardian Angel. The Mangler himself, an altered character, was setting them to work, his chin freshly shaved
and an angelic smile on his face, a thing which the oldest
inhabitants of the shanty-town had never seen in their
lives before.

In the twinkling of an eye the Champs-Elysées and the
alleys leading off it had a brand-new tarmac surface. The
rickety, tumble-down shacks were transformed into neat
bungalows, each surrounded by a green lawn. The Wadi
Radam now ran openly through the village with swans
swimming on its limpid waters. Flowers and shrubs grew
all over the place. In an instant men, women and children
cast off their old ragged clothes and stood smartly dressed
from head to foot. Bofano's grocery swelled to four times
its size and became an ultra-modern self-service store,
bulging with goods at give-away prices. This wave of the
magic wand affected even Fat Théo's ill-famed canteen,
reducing it to ashes and causing to spring up in its place a
snack-bar with plate-glass windows, piped music and
pretty waitresses.

Lying in his narrow bed, Cady watched the miracle
grow and spread and he waited now for the triumphal

moment when the walls of the Green House tumbled down. What fairy palace would rise to replace them?

A key grated in a lock and the noise put his dreams to flight without fully waking him. He wondered whether it was Monsieur Langelin or Madame Meunier, as he kept his eyes tight shut to preserve some of the wonder of the dream until the last possible moment. Then the dog beside him began to growl, and furtive steps made for the corner of the surgery.

It was a terrible effort to force his eyes open, but when he did, Cady confidently expected to see the Guardian Angel smiling in amusement and holding a cup of hot coffee. Instead looming over him he saw the fearful face of the Mangler, his hat pulled down to his bushy black eyebrows, his eyes unblinking and cold as glass, his thick-lipped mouth closed over the stub of a cigar.

'What the hell are you doing in here?' the Scrap-metal King asked.

'I'm the school caretaker,' Cady stuttered. 'Monsieur Langelin lets me kip down on this camp bed. I was asleep.'

The Mangler scowled at the bare walls with their tiny windows, the pupils' benches, the teacher's desk of scrubbed deal and the grey metal cupboard in which Madame Meunier kept her first-aid equipment and her medicines.

'What are you taking care of?' he guffawed. 'I can't see anything valuable in this rotten shack.'

'It's the cleanest place in the village,' Cady said deliberately. 'And because it's clean it's worth more than anything to the fifty children who take shelter here every morning.'

He tied up his foot-cloths, one eye on the dictator, and then swung his feet to the ground to put on his new boots. All his confidence returned at once. Pignouf had crawled under the bed. He was still growling and his lips were

76

curled back to expose a respectable set of teeth. This threat annoyed their visitor.

'Make that dog shut up, or he'll get a taste of my boot.'

'This is his place,' Cady retorted cheekily. 'If you don't like it you can always get out.'

The Mangler's heavy hand caught him full in the face and sent him crashing to the floor. Pignouf sprang from hiding and treacherously attacked the attacker from behind. The Mangler began to spin like a top, kicking out wildly to make him let go of his leg.

'Call that hound of yours off!' he yelled. 'Or I'll empty my pistol in his guts!'

Suddenly a shrill whistle came from up in the roof. Pignouf leaped aside and dived under the bed once more. Cady was lying beside the medicine cupboard, blood streaming down his face. Painfully he sat up and wiped his mouth with the back of his hand. The Mangler got his breath back and looked round in bewilderment.

'Who whistled?'

'Wasn't me,' said Cady. 'The dog was all ready to take a good mouthful out of your ankles. I wish he'd gone ahead.'

'Want another clout?'

'You won't touch me, not now you won't.'

Supporting himself on the cupboard, he struggled to his feet and grabbed a stool in both hands to bring the odds more in his favour. There was a second whistle from above them. The Mangler looked up and spotted the black bird perched above the doorway.

'No fighting in Mother Dutilleul's place!' Igor exclaimed. 'You start that again, my old fruit, and I'll call the cops!'

He flapped his wings and underlined the threat with another piercing whistle. The Scrap-metal King stood still.

'That's the first time I've ever come across a crow that can talk. Who does it belong to?'

'Nobody for the moment. He just breezed in. Someone must have been boasting about your shanty-town to him. If you ask me, we're wrong to call him a common-or-garden crow.'

'He called me an old fruit,' the Mangler retorted, very much on his dignity. 'One good turn deserves another. What's his name?'

'He generally introduces himself,' Cady replied.

'Well, you old crook, aren't you going to say hullo to Igor?' the bird croaked, and waddled along the beam.

The Mangler opened his mouth to give as good an insult as he had got, when he was diverted from this task by the racket of a 2 CV coming down the track and pulling up outside the Green House with a squeal of brakes.

A moment later Madame Meunier pushed the door wide open and stopped at the threshold on catching sight of Public Enemy Number One. She was a little woman in a drab old coat, but her skinny cheeks flushed pink with anger.

'Who said you could come in?'

'I don't need to ask,' the Mangler sneered. 'I'm at home anywhere in Bois-Bréau.'

'He's got a duplicate key,' Cady explained. 'Like the gipsies . . . He came sneaking in and gave me a clout on the nose for my breakfast.'

'That was the dog's fault,' the Scrap-metal King explained with a shifty grin. 'If he'd wanted a bone, he shouldn't have chosen my legs.'

From beneath the camp-bed Pignouf started to growl again, while from his vantage-point Igor flapped his wings and gave a prolonged whistle. Cady had kept hold of his stool and now he moved stealthily to bring the green hat well within range. He was not going to miss so tempting a target.

'Out you go!' Madame Meunier calmly announced as she marched straight up to the colossus.

'I'll have what you owe me first!' the Mangler retorted. 'I'm not having you feed these brats on my rent money. Three months' arrears, that's a hundred and fifty francs. Hand it over!'

'Don't you pay,' said Cady. 'You don't owe him anything.'

Pignouf stuck his hairy muzzle out from under the bed and began to bark fiercely. Igor whistled and chirruped wildly from his beam.

'No fighting in Mother Dutilleul's place or I'll call the cops!'

'Belt up!' the Mangler yelled at him, losing his temper.

'In my own good time!' the black bird replied. 'You come over here, you fat sack of guts, and we'll settle this man to man!'

'I want my money!' yelled the Scrap-metal King.

'Don't you pay!' Cady told Madame Meunier once again. 'Please don't pay.'

But the uproar made her head throb and she gave in for the sake of a little peace and quiet. From his wind-cheater the Mangler drew a thick bundle of greasy, dirty notes and slipped into it the money offered to him at arm's length. With supreme satisfaction he put the whole lot back into his pocket.

'You've done the right and proper thing,' he told them cheerfully. 'Everyone has been refusing to pay me their rent and I was beginning to wonder where the revolt had started. Now that they know you've settled your arrears, my debtors will change their tune.'

Furtively his cold eyes glanced left and right, peering at the weak woman who stood facing him and at the ragged

79

boy innocently clutching a stool. There was nothing unusual about the boy except the rubber boots he was wearing, their tan a perfect imitation leather.

'I've never had much gratitude from Bois-Bréau,' the scrap-merchant went on. 'I know I'm called the Mangler. Why, I ask you? I went to the trouble of levelling the ground, putting in foundations and timber, and it cost me a lot of money. My men were decent enough to run a pipe from the reservoir to the village and put in the wiring so you've got street lighting.'

'You got your money back in six months,' Madame Meunier told him coldly. 'Anyway, you don't even own the land.'

'I chose the site myself to improve the lot of the worker. They've only to cross the road and they're on the site. No lost time: no fares to pay. That's a consideration, isn't it? The only thing that was missing was a cosy spot where they could meet their pals and have a quiet drink. So, of course, I had to open that quiet little canteen which their hooligan kids wrecked the other morning.'

'The place is run by three brutes who terrorise Bois-Bréau when the women are left on their own,' Madame Meunier replied. 'The boys and girls may have reacted somewhat explosively, but you and your men set them an example of violence on every occasion.'

'It won't happen again,' the Mangler hissed. 'I'll look after that side of things myself.'

'I'm not so sure as you are. Now that bridge has been crossed, the slightest step you take in that direction will bring the same response.'

'We'll see about that!'

'It's been seen about already,' Cady muttered as he sniffed back the blood in his nose.

'I'll warm your ears for you!' the Mangler threatened.

'You'll get this stool in your face first.'

Bravely Madame Meunier was forced to intervene and to shepherd the lad into the far corner of the surgery. With a crude gesture the Mangler spat the butt of his cigar on the floor and his frosty glance fell once more on the tan boots of his opponent.

'They cost you a packet?' he asked with a honeyed smile.

'Just a sprint up the road. They were a housewarming-present when I first came to Bois-Bréau.'

'I wouldn't say too much about them, if I were you,' chuckled the Scrap-metal King. 'They caught my eye the other morning. Someone could well pay a lot for them.'

'In cash?' Cady asked.

'With his skin,' the Mangler replied, turning to go. 'With his skin and his job.'

He vanished in the murky light of the village, leaving the threat hanging in the air. Madame Meunier gave a deep sigh and came over to Cady.

'Let's give your nose some first aid to start with,' she murmured. 'Did he punch you in the face?'

'No, just slapped me, but it was as hard as a punch.'

'Well, did you deserve it?'

'Perhaps I did.' Cady shrugged. 'I couldn't help myself when I saw that villain. And I felt safer in the Green House than anywhere else.'

Very gently Madame Meunier washed his face and cleaned his nostrils with two pieces of cotton-wool soaked in antiseptic. This made Cady's eyes water for a minute or two, but he soon recovered his cheerful grin.

'We'll have some coffee soon,' she told him. 'But we must unload the car first.'

Cady helped her carry in the churns of milk and the long loaves of bread stacked on the back seat.

'Would you like me to get rid of the dog?' was the next thing he asked her. 'You can't blame him for having

81

bitten the Mangler, but I don't want him to use this as an excuse for hanging around the place.'

Pignouf wagged his stub of a tail, and ducked his head as Madame Meunier's eyes smiled at him.

'He can stay until the little ones come,' she agreed. 'Monsieur Langelin would be cross with me if I sent him away without any breakfast. And then, he *is* the only dog in Bois-Bréau. He deserves something, if he has been able to survive all that ill-treatment.'

She lit the gas to heat the coffee.

Meanwhile Cady was worrying about the black bird. He could hear it moving and muttering to itself in the gloom up in the roof. Madame Meunier had not dared complain, but he was sure she dreaded the sound of that voice which had joined in the discussion a few moments before. After all, she did not deserve to be called an old fruit or to hear the ill-educated creature demand a stiff Pernod at eight in the morning.

Cady looked up and gave a friendly whistle. With a whirr of wings, Igor fluttered down from his beam and alighted on the finger held out for him. Madame Meunier looked up from the coffee on the stove. She kept absolutely quiet.

Igor turned an inquisitive beak in her direction. Cady was on tenterhooks, for he would have liked to have undertaken the introductions himself, if only to cut short the flow of nonsense. But the crew of the grey lorry had taught their mascot manners and the black bird took the lead.

'Good morning, madame!' he said ceremoniously. 'My name's Igor . . . '

He waggled his tail several times in greeting as Madame Meunier came over with a smile on her face.

'Say hullo and ask him how he is,' Cady hissed. 'Then you'll be friends for life.'

82

'Hullo, Igor . . . How are you this morning?'

'Not too bad,' the bird replied. 'But my stomach's been flapping against my backbone for the last forty miles and I hope we're going to stop for a bite soon. Eight hours on the road certainly does give you an appetite!'

'The coffee's boiling,' said Madame Meunier. 'What will you have?'

'The usual: beer for the boys and a good stiff Pernod for . . .'

'Igor! Remember your manners!' Cady spoke to him severely.

Igor hung his head in shame and with two flutters of his wings flew onto his young master's shoulder.

'Can you stroke him?' Madame Meunier asked.

'I don't know. We only found him last night and we don't dare to frighten him.'

He told her all about the bird's arrival and the way in which he had made himself at home in Bois-Bréau. The close watch which the children of the shanty-town were keeping on the Mangler and his accomplices frightened Madame Meunier.

'I don't blame you for acting as you've done, since you've got right on your side. But do be careful, and don't pry too deeply into what they're doing. Our neighbours are unscrupulous as well as crooked. Do you suppose a type like the Mangler would think twice about killing to protect his interests? Of course he wouldn't. And who would bother about one child more or less in Bois-Bréau?'

Igor began to beat his wings against Cady's shoulder and to shriek,

'The Mangler! . . . The Mangler! . . . We'll stand up to him all right. I'll call Charlie and old Gaston to the rescue and then you'll see some fun . . . Go to it, lads. Put your foot down: only another hundred miles to Perpignan!'

Cheered by the interruption, they returned to the Green House's latest guest.

'Is he a blackbird? Is he a crow?' Cady asked. 'We hadn't a clue.'

'Neither,' said Madame Meunier as she took a closer look at the bird. 'He's a myna. That's a sort of thrush from India, which can talk as well as a parrot and has an even more amazing memory.'

'Clever?'

'That depends on the company he keeps.'

'Then Charlie and Gaston must have been a right pair.'

'Where have my two mates gone?' Igor croaked in his ear.

'You should know,' the boy replied.

'Into Mother Dutilleul's place for a bite to eat.' Igor reeled it off.

'And while they were there their lorry was pinched.'

There was dead silence. Madame Meunier gave Cady a scared look.

'Keep out of this business. Tell Sandra I told you so. She's the eldest and she'll understand.'

'But the fun's started now,' Cady objected. 'And since we all think it is fun, let's keep it going until it blows up. What's the risk at Bois-Bréau?'

'Here come the cops,' Igor shouted. 'Pull in and let the highway patrol go through!'

His red beak swung round to the half-open door. The track resounded to the roar of a motor-scooter.

Laden like a mule, Monsieur Langelin soon appeared in the doorway. One glance was enough for him to take in the scene: the dog lolling on the bed, Madame Meunier pouring boiling water on to her coffee-grounds and the orphan boy shaking his finger at a bundle of black feathers perched on his shoulder.

'Lord!' he exclaimed, dropping his parcels on the floor.

'A bird was the one thing this soul-less house needed, and this one certainly isn't a dove of peace.'

'Wotcher, me old cock!' Igor called out to him. 'Forgetting your old friends these days?'

Madame Meunier choked back her laughter, while Cady hid his face and tried to get rid of the bird which clutched his sweater. But the monster kept its hold and chattered happily away, oblivious of whom he was addressing.

The silence and unconcern of the Guardian Angel at last exhausted the chatterbox and all was calm once more when Madame Meunier served coffee. Once she had made the necessary introductions, she went on to tell of the Mangler's visit and what it had cost the community chest. Monsieur Langelin did not blame her.

'I would have done the same thing myself, out of a wish to be honest,' was all he said, 'but the money that's just melted into that wretched man's pocket means about five days' rations lost, without taking into account that we're getting more and more children every morning now that the weather's turning colder. How can we make it up?'

'If the scrap-metal market's on the up and up,' Cady suggested, 'maybe he'd have a change of heart and bring back the money himself.'

'You don't know that shark yet. A real villain as well as a miser. He hardly ever pays his accomplices and only holds them together by a mixture of threats and promises. He counts every penny, and he's made a fortune out of five hundred homeless people in under two years . . . I'm entirely in agreement with Madame Meunier—so long as he, either personally or through his strong-arm men, takes no action against the people who are standing up to him, you are to leave him alone and stop spying on him.'

But that was just what Zalko and his brother were

doing through the windows of their parents' caravan. Twenty minutes before, they had watched the Mangler go down to the village in the grey light of dawn, and then enter like a thief the Green House which the children of Bois-Bréau regarded as a sanctuary nobody could violate.

'Neither the Guardian Angel nor the lady are there yet,' Zalko told his young brother. 'There's just Cady and the dog. If those two show their teeth, they're going to get flattened. Pignouf's all skin and bone and hardly has the strength to stand up.'

A little later the arrival of Madame Meunier relieved some of their anxiety. It was growing lighter outside and the housewives were heading for Bofano's grocery with their milk jugs.

'Are we going to take a look?' Zalko's brother asked.

'When we hear a shout for help, not before,' Zalko answered.

At last the Mangler came out of the Green House and made his way up the track with the rolling gait of a bear. He spat scornfully into the gipsies' camp and walked straight back to his scrap-yard, just as the Dormouse returned from Mareuil with a bundle under his arm—the morning papers. From that moment things in the enemy camp really started to go wrong.

The first thing which the Zalko brothers noticed was that the opponents of the evening before had made it up during the night, for they were swapping jokes as they lounged about at the far end of the yard. All talk stopped the instant the boss returned. As he approached, the Mangler had been opening the papers one after the other, feverishly turning the pages in search of a particular item, stopping short to read a dozen lines or so, and then crumpling the paper up and hurling it away in a rage. The others seemed appalled. Finally he barked an order and the entire gang followed him into the office-building.

86

The meeting lasted about half an hour. Then the men who worked the hydraulic press and the foundrymen hurried out and back to their workshops at the far end of the scrap-yard. Next came the strong-arm men, Big Jules and Old Fred at their head, making for the sheds to the right. Finally, out came the Mangler and the Crocodile, each swinging a long and heavy wooden club. The scrap-merchant's white Chevrolet was still parked in its old place and Filochard, who was polishing it, watched the two men as they opened the gate and then stared for some time down the road towards the mist-shrouded cross-roads.

'I bet they're coming back to the village,' said Zalko suddenly. 'You stay here while I warn the others.'

Meanwhile time had passed and the Green House had been slowly filling up, until now it re-echoed to the singing of the children. Mourab and Taëb kept watch outside.

'Sandra's inside with her mates,' they told the gipsy. 'The Spaniards and the Portuguese are there too . . . If you've come for the grub, you're too late. It's been dished out.'

The hinges squealed as Zalko forced the door open. His entry interrupted the song of the choir conducted by Monsieur Langelin.

'The Mangler and the Crocodile are heading for the village!' he announced. 'And they've got their coshes with them . . .'

'Then we'd better watch out,' Sandra said and rose to her feet.

Her friends followed suit at once and clustered round the door. The Guardian Angel still clutched his guitar.

'Sit where you are and let them come. The last thing you should do is provoke them . . . Now, you others,' he said, turning towards the little ones, 'let's have that third verse:

87

'In the greenwood tree
'A nightingale was singing . . . '

He plucked once more at his guitar in fine style, tapping his desk with his left foot to give them the rhythm. The youthful choir burst into song once more and their shrill voices filled the chilly walls of the Green House. Madame Meunier was at the opposite end of the building with her dress-making class around her, and she imagined for a moment that the gentle little song would turn aside the storm. Two verses of its sad refrain fled amid the shadows up in the roof:

'I have loved you long,
'And never will forget you . . . '

This was the moment which the Mangler chose for his entrance with his personal strong-arm man, opening the door in his own inimitable fashion, that is, by setting his foot to it and pushing with such force that it slammed hard against the wall. This thunder-clap rocked the Green House on its foundations and stopped the song in the choristers' throats. Two burly figures walked in side by side, their clubs under their right arms.

'You've no business to come in here!' Monsieur Langelin shouted at them from his desk. 'You've had your money, haven't you? Then leave us in peace. This is the children's own place—their school. The only concern of Madame Meunier and myself is to look after them, teach them and amuse them. If one of you dares lift a finger against them it will cost you far more than mere trespass!'

'Mind your own business!' the Crocodile retorted rudely. 'We couldn't care less about these snotty-nosed brats! Teach them what nonsense you please and just keep out of our way! We're here to collect something that belongs to us, that's all.'

The Guardian Angel picked up his guitar once more

and without a tremor struck a few chords, an introduction which they quickly understood. Once the first shock was over, the small singers quickly recovered. They all took a deep breath to break into a children's song as old, but far gayer than the first:

> 'The ferret, the ferret,
> 'From Bois-Joli,
> 'Runs hither and thither,
> 'So nosey is he.'

Sandra then gave the sign and the bigger ones joined their deeper voices to the trebles. The excitement of these goings-on made them sing horribly out of tune, but they brought into the song a subtle change of wording:

> 'The blackbird, the blackbird,
> 'From Bois-Bréau,
> 'Flies hither and thither,
> "Cos he's in the know.'

The music was a marvellous accompaniment to the extraordinary behaviour of their visitors, whose first action was to walk from one end of the room to the other peering under the seats and desks. Next they opened the Guardian Angel's cardboard cartons and the medicine cupboard, and poked with their clubs among the school equipment stacked behind the master's desk. All this was done with a haste and nervousness which did not improve their general appearance. Having found nothing, they then began to peer up into the dim recesses of the roof and to whistle with an assumed gentleness to tempt the ferret of Bois-Joli to show them his nose.

There was no response. In the end the Crocodile hurled his club with all his might between the beams. There was a tremendous boom as the cosh hit the corrugated iron and then it came down like a boomerang, hitting him right on the top of the head. To the delight of the audience he burst into a flood of curses.

'We aren't in the circus!' the Mangler thundered as he brought his club crashing down on the master's desk.

His bellow brought the song of the ferret to an end and checked the wave of titters which was beginning to spread from bench to bench. All that could be heard was a whirring sound coming from floor-level in perfect imitation of the sound the mocking bird made when it flew. Ali and Saïd Boubarka, however, stopped rubbing their boots together as soon as they saw the intruders go down on all fours in the centre aisle once more. They were soon up on their feet again, breathless and glaring angrily.

'Where's that bird?' the Mangler panted, when all was still again.

His question made the little ones smile. They had not the remotest idea what this interlude was all about. Their Guardian Angel meanwhile had put down his guitar and very calmly replied:

'What bird are you talking about?'

'There was one in the building a little whiie ago when I came to collect my money from the nurse . . . Where have you hidden it?'

Monsieur Langelin put on an expression of utter bewilderment and turned to the toddlers.

'Did any of you see a bird when you came into the Green House?'

No! They had seen the village dog, Pignouf, run cowering away with a piece of bread in his mouth. They had seen Madame Meunier buttering slices of bread and filling cups with malted milk. They had seen the new boy, the one who could put back dislocated joints and cure sprains. But they hadn't seen any bird!

The Mangler was beside himself and his red-rimmed eyes looked daggers at his audience. At last, among those fifty grubby faces he caught sight of the young joker who claimed to be the caretaker of this rickety wooden hut of a school.

Cady let himself be hauled from his place like a rag doll.

'You were here when I first came,' said the Mangler. 'And so was that bird. You saw him and heard him as plainly as I did. It's a chatter-box of a bird . . . where is it now?'

'I don't know,' Cady replied, unconcerned. 'Igor's free to come and go as he likes. I'm not his owner. When the class started, he flew out of the door. Nobody turned him out.'

'Which way did he go?'

'I didn't notice . . . If he belongs to you, there's no need to worry, Igor will come home to roost sooner or later. He's only got to cross the road. If he's not yours, that's a different matter. We'll have to take his word for it. But there it is! Do we have to take everything he says at face value?'

The Mangler, his hat jammed down on his forehead, sweated and pulled a face. There was no hint of mockery in the boy's fluting voice, but matters had reached a crisis point at which its very seriousness suddenly became sarcasm.

'What do you mean, "everything he says"?'

'Igor didn't tell me where he was going,' Cady admitted. 'But ever since yesterday he's been asking me to take him out for a drink. What he misses is a good stiff Pernod in front of him and his mates around him. This isn't a lot, but it is a possible clue to his owner.'

'Are you having me on?' the Mangler growled.

'No, I'm not. All I'm trying to do is get a little sense out of what that bird's been jabbering about. As far as I can see the only place round here where he's likely to get a snifter of Pernod is the canteen, and the only person kind enough to give him one on tick is Fat Théo!'

The Scrap-metal King and his Crocodile dived out of the door to escape the hoots of laughter which suddenly shook the Green House.

The Guardian Angel raised his eyes and tapped his fingers on the guitar.

'Let's have it again!' he said calmly. 'One, two, three . . .'

The raucous choir of big and small burst once more into song:

> 'The blackbird, the blackbird,
> 'From Bois-Bréau,
> 'Flies hither and thither,
> ''Cos he's in the know.'

Enthusiastically Sandra and the boys repeated the verse and then left the Green House without a word to their Guardian Angel.

'We'll keep up with the hunt as close as we can,' she told the others. 'We certainly aren't going to miss the fun . . . Do you think they'll catch Igor?'

'I bet they won't,' Cady shouted as he took to his heels.

6

The Bird in the Bar

LIKE ALL the children in the shanty-town, Violet and
Rosie wore the oldest of sweaters which had been
patched and darned twenty times over and jeans
which had been cut down to fit them. All the same,
the ribbons, which were the only way of telling one
from the other, were always dazzlingly clean and tied
in neat bows in hair which was as carefully brushed
and combed.

They had been missing that morning when the gang
first rallied, as they usually did, on the corner outside
Bofano's grocery. First of all they had had carefully to dig
up the geranium growing outside their door, and then
they had had to pot it in the lean-to beside their shack.
There had been a thin coat of frost on the roadside and
Madame Belin dreaded what the winter might do to the
solitary plant which gave so many flowers during the
summer.

Once they had done this, the two little girls came down
the alley and emerged on to the muck of the Champs-
Elysées where the mud had hardened overnight. Fog still
cloaked this scene of desolation. Not many people were
about; only the silent housewives plodding towards the
grocery and a few toddlers, swathed in scarves, playing
beside the Wadi Radam, and the dog Pignouf seeking a
pat or a bone from door to door.

The twins were on the point of heading for the Green
House when two burly figures came hurrying down the

street, swung sharply off to the left and went into the canteen.

'Fat Théo's got important customers!' said Violet to her sister. 'The Mangler and the Crocodile . . . That doesn't sound too good. I hope the look-out at the end of the street saw them and Sandra knows what's going on.'

Their curiosity made them follow. They stepped on to the duckboards outside the canteen and without making a sound peered through the half-open window. They could only see a tiny bit of the dimly-lighted room, but what they could hear was very funny indeed.

'What bird?' Fat Théo was asking as he scratched his head. 'I opened up at the usual time. The only people we've seen so far are a couple of out-of-work Italians. They each had a coffee with a dash of rum in it and left without paying.'

'I expect the boss means that Polish bachelor we chucked out and who kept asking us for his furniture,' Spud said. 'No, he hasn't come back again since last Thursday. Battling Flagada put him down for the count.'

The old boxer stuck out his chest in his thick red polo-necked sweater, clenching and unclenching his enormous fists.

'A left hook! Just one left hook! That was enough to teach him.'

'Shut up and listen, you thick-headed louts!' the Mangler yelled, quivering with rage. 'I'm not talking about a fellow, I'm talking about a bird, a real live bird!'

Fat Théo and his attendants looked at one another and across their faces flickered a momentary doubt—Horace Kovacovici had gone slightly crazy this morning.

'We haven't seen your bird,' the bartender said, humouring him. 'Or perhaps it's come into the room without our noticing it . . . First of all, what sort of a bird is it?'

94

'I don't quite know,' the Mangler answered impatiently. 'I only saw it in the distance. It's black all over and about as big as a crow or a large blackbird. But the thing about my bird, you thick-headed lout, is that it talks the same as you and me!'

'You don't say!'

'Why, it can even join in a conversation.'

'What does it talk about?'

'Odds and ends of this and that. But if they find it here, we're finished, so at all costs we've got to catch it and wring its neck before anyone gets to hear of it.'

'When?'

'Today, because one solitary feather is enough to bring the cops into Bois-Bréau by the score ... I suppose you wouldn't mind having to close down your bar?'

Théo concealed his embarrassment, but it was a hard job. He was becoming convinced that the Scrap-metal King had gone stark raving mad.

'No! Honestly! We haven't seen it ... Anyway, what would a bird want to come into a bar for?'

'The same as anyone else, for a drink.'

The three toughs looked at one another once more with glazed eyes.

'You're joking, boss,' Spud stuttered.

The Mangler quivered even more.

'Haven't you seen the papers? My crow has three whole columns to himself ... and he's got his picture on the front page, too.'

The Crocodile produced a paper from his leather jacket, opened it and handed it to the staff of the 'Eldorado'. Soon they were deep in it.

The door to the foggy street had remained ajar. Not one of them heard a soft rustle in the threshold.

'Now do you understand, you thick-headed louts?' the Mangler asked them when they had finished. 'It's a bird that's set in his ways: he follows his masters wherever they go . . . '

'Even when they pop in for a drink.' A deep voice came from the end of the room. 'That surprise you, me old fruits? Whose turn is it to buy a round? What's your poison? Igor will have his usual stiff Pernod, but just one! Drink up and go!'

All five looked up with a start. The demon of Bois-Bréau was perched on the topmost shelf behind the bar, flapping his stumpy wings in utter scorn for his peril. The Crocodile's cosh flashed like a thunderbolt and shattered a score of bottles which fell behind the bar.

'Good shot!' shouted the Mangler. 'You got him this time!'

The myna had vanished. They crowded into the narrow space to finish him off as he lay, a still ball of feathers, amid the broken glass.

'I've got him,' said Fat Théo. 'I didn't think he was real, but I've got him now. Give me my cosh and I'll make mincemeat of him.'

He had not even time to bend down. With a whirr Igor darted between his legs, gained the door in a series of short bursts of flight, shot under the bewildered faces of the twins and promptly disappeared into the yellowish fog which cloaked the shanty-town.

The Mangler heaved a deep sigh and clenched his teeth to control his rage.

'In his condition,' the Crocodile told him, 'that bird's not going to get very far. All we've got to do is scout round the alleys one by one, like we do on our monthly inspections. You three, shut the bar and get off down to the Wadi Radam right away. You're going to be our beaters.'

They split up at the door of the 'Eldorado' without noticing any suspicious movement in the vicinity, but every so often a grubby-faced innocent standing by his hovel would let one of them come up to him.

'You haven't seen a black bird around here, have you? With drooping wings?' the Crocodile asked in a smooth voice.

Beppo Torrente silently pointed up at the galvanised metal cage hanging above the shattered door. In it hopped a naked, songless canary. The eviction of the other morning had stopped his tongue for good and all.

As they came back along the Wadi Radam, waving their clubs, the only game the two toughs started was a pair of rats which they surprised at the mouth of the drain. Patiently the Mangler explored the alleys in the French end of the village, behind Bofano's grocery. A chorus of whistles caught his attention and suddenly he came upon Pimpin Léonard and Mimile Rouvier sitting in the middle of the road examining a hefty crow which they were just about to pluck.

'Where did you catch him?' asked the Mangler in a crazy burst of optimism.

'In the bushes on the slope above the Belins' shack.'

'Did he say anything to you?'

Pimpin burst out laughing.

'Not a croak out of him! He's been dead four or five days. Touch him! Hard as iron ... Mimile's granny's going to try and make him into soup.'

Horace heard another whistle, this time from inside the shack. He shoved the door open, stepped inside and then backed out again fast.

'Out!' Madame Rouvier shouted at him, brandishing her largest frying-pan.

She might be an old bag of bones, but under that patient exterior was a redoubtable strength of character. The Mangler left the old crow-eater to her kitchen and went on his way.

Two figures were standing at the end of the alley looking towards the stunted bushes which had once been the Bois-Bréau. Sneaking up on them, he saw that one was the tall brown-haired girl who had made a name for herself a few days before by leading a rebellion without precedent in the history of the shanty-town. She wore a woollen cap pulled down over her dark hair, an ancient cast-off black coat of her grandfather's and the inevitable jeans stuffed into dilapidated wellingtons.

Beside her stood the boy from the Green House, about whom even the inhabitants of the Casbah told such wonderful things, because his supple fingers healed the sprains of the labourers on the Plastorex site. Of all unlikely stories! In any case he'd just had the best clout for many a long day, so that his upper lip was still marked and swollen.

'What are you looking at?'

They hardly moved a muscle. Cady simply stood aside to let the lord of the manor pass between him and his friend. Their faces were pinched with cold, but neither showed a trace of fear, for in the right hand each held a stout lath studded with nails—as deadly a weapon as the Mangler's own cosh.

Sandra pointed to the leafless bushes.

'Birds,' she muttered. 'Can't you hear them?'

From this distance nothing could be seen, but a chorus of chirping came from beneath the branches white with frost.

'Sparrows,' she said again, 'and a few blackbirds. They're upset by this first frost and are getting ready to fly away. Most of them will roost under the eaves of Mareuil or Sartrouville, and the rest in the Forest of Saint-Germain. Our houses are too cold and they won't find many crumbs along the Champs-Elysées!'

The Mangler said nothing, but slowly forced his way

into the bushes and turned over the dead leaves. He seemed bewitched by the chirping of the birds.

'Looking for something?' Sandra called to him in a friendly voice. 'If you'd like a sparrow-hunt, our mates would love to give you a hand . . . You just say the word and we'll all come running.'

There was no reply. Then from the Portuguese end of the village came the Crocodile, with Fat Théo and his two gorillas close behind. They tiptoed up to the Mangler and listened carefully to his instructions. The birds chirruped and sang in the undergrowth. The five men scattered to form a line a few yards from where they had been standing. The Scrap-metal King gave the signal and they all plunged into the bushes hitting out wildly with their clubs. Bois-Bréau was suddenly a prodigious mass of beating wings. The blackbirds, being more wary, had already fluttered away, but the rest of the flock scattered in all directions twittering angrily.

Sandra and Cady laughed until they cried.

'The rest of the gang shouldn't miss this,' the boy said.

A long-drawn whistle brought the other watchers from their hiding-places and attracted about fifty children to the edge of the wood. The lunatic hunters went on striking out in a blind frenzy and sent the dead leaves whirling in clouds around them.

'I've got a couple!' Fat Théo shouted. 'A big one and a little one . . . '

'I've got five or six!' added the Crocodile. 'One of them's alive still.'

'Can he talk?' asked the Mangler.

'After the crack I've given him, it would be a wonder if he could. But I think he looks like the one in the canteen.'

'Let me see.'

They arranged their bag in a row on the frosty turf. It amounted in all to a score of unfortunate small birds crushed by their blows. The Mangler looked long and carefully at them, but drew no conclusions from what he saw.

'Let's carry on a bit further,' he said in disappointment.

They scattered like skirmishers and beat on another hundred yards through the undergrowth. Behind them Sandra led the sparrows of Bois-Bréau. They were not going to miss a second of this; it was hilarious.

'A thousand francs for the one who catches my bird!' the Mangler called to raise the spirits of his men.

They managed to put up a solitary rook, which flapped away from its perch croaking disgustedly. By now the bushes were beginning to thin and they could see the distant chimneys of Nanterre poking through the fog. There wasn't a bird left, except at the edge of the shanty-town, in a few neglected thickets into which their imitators plunged joyously.

In the end they had to stop when they reached the marshes of Argenteuil, a desolate expanse of swamp and wasteland stretching to the wall of the Radam Works. A thousand crows or more flapped and strutted across this waste. The sight of these birds depressed the hunters' spirits altogether.

'There's no point in going on.' The Mangler made up his mind. 'Let's get back to the village and pretend nothing has been happening. The talking bird can't have left the place. Keep your eyes open, lads, the reward still stands . . . If we have to, we'll visit every single one of their stinking shacks.'

After the five of them had got together again they made a long detour through the woods to avoid attention and crept back through the end of the village where the Negroes lived, but it was wasted effort. Swallowing their rage, they came down the Champs-Elysées to the accompaniment of bird-calls, despite the fact that the doors were closed, there was not a light in the windows and the village looked deserted.

'Shall I go and get my rifle?' the Crocodile asked.

The Mangler shook his head.

'That's the last thing I want you to do. You couldn't have thought of anything riskier. No, all I want is a couple of volunteers to go and search the Casbah.'

Neither Fat Théo nor his attendants moved.

'You useless, gutless lot!' the Mangler roared. 'There was that bird, made its nest among the bottles in the bar, and you didn't even notice it! I should have all three of you back in the scrap-yard.'

'We didn't know about it,' Spud pleaded. 'He should have ordered his Pernod sooner. I can tell you he'd have had it right away.'

His joke made them all laugh and the tension relaxed.

'After all the excitement, what we need is a drink,' the Mangler said, and wiped the sweat from his face. 'Then I can get some of the lads from the yard, like Old Fred and his mob, and we can start the hunt up again with me in charge. I've simply got to get that bird, you hear?'

They had stopped singing in the Green House and for the last moment or two had been listening to the Guardian Angel's clear voice giving his version of one of the Gospel stories. Sandra opened the door slowly so that it would not creak too much, ushered her friends in and quietly sat down with them in the back row. Quiet as they had been, the story-teller noticed their arrival. He stopped, but did not seem in the least annoyed.

'Did they get him?' he asked eagerly.

All heads turned as one to the back row.

'They've just come back empty-handed,' Sandra answered. 'Our bird's still on the wing, but it was a near-miss for him and for us, too. Can you imagine it?

The Mangler and the Crocodile drove him out from behind the bottles in the canteen! The twins were there and saw it all.'

'Well, I never!' Monsieur Langelin pretended to be shocked. 'And does he drink as much as he talks, then?'

'He's just shooting a line,' Cady replied. 'I'm sure Igor's never dipped his beak in a glass of Pernod in his life.'

'Where is he now?' Madame Meunier asked, when the laughter had died down.

'We haven't a clue,' Sandra said. 'There's no sign of him in the village, but we've passed the word round, and if anyone sees or hears him, they'll let us know at once.'

Monsieur Langelin had lost the thread of his story, so he brought the proceedings to a close with an announcement which raised shouts of delight from his audience.

'Because of the cold, we'll go back to our winter programme. From today, the house will be open every afternoon until five o'clock and we shall have a snack and a hot drink for you. We should like each of you to bring a little bit of fuel to keep the stove going. I'm not asking you to pull the door down or take the roof off: a handful of dead twigs will do, or a few old planks or even some sawdust.'

'I'll bring you whatever you want,' Simbad called cheekily. 'I'll even nick the duckboards in front of the canteen from under Théo's nose.'

'I'm not having any trouble with Théo,' Monsieur Langelin laughed. 'Why don't you try to dig out the surviving tree-stumps in Bois-Bréau? Once they'd dried out, they'd go like a bomb.'

And then, in a flash, the room emptied, Madame Meunier departed in her 2 CV, and the Green House was left to its Guardian Angel. First, he rearranged the desks,

102

then put the games back in their box, piled the books on the teacher's desk and finally swept the centre aisle. When this task was done, he was by the open door.

Someone was sitting in the gloom at the end of the back bench. Monsieur Langelin heard a cough, looked round and at once recognised the red woollen jerkin which was unlike anything else in Bois-Bréau.

'Nobody's invited you to dinner, then? You're out of luck.'

'I'm not hungry,' Cady answered.

'Liar! Light Madame Meunier's stove. I'll open a tin of meat to go on our bread and we'll have a bowl of soup as well. . . . And now shut that door.'

Cady did not move. His head was on one side and he seemed to be listening to some angelic voice coming from the roof. Monsieur Langelin propped his broom against the wall and shut the door himself. He was worried to see Cady sitting so still.

'Is anything the matter?'

The boy grinned, then pursed his lips and whistled softly in an ascending scale—*doh, ray, me*—which rose to the roof in friendly invitation. The bird was there, hiding in a dark corner. At once he flew down and perched on Cady's shoulder.

'I never thought we'd see him again!' Monsieur Langelin was pleased at the return of the prodigal. 'How ever did he manage to get in?'

'I expect when we did, just before midday. He was lying in the gutter on the edge of the roof with his head hanging down and his wings spread out, like one of the birds the Mangler's men slaughtered. I didn't want to say anything to the others because I thought he was dead. But he wasn't, he was just waiting for the door to open. Hullo, Igor!'

The bird did not deign to answer. With the tip of his

beak he was preening his dusty wings and cleaning the sticky vermouth and anis from his breast feathers.

'Another time,' Cady said, 'he'll think twice before he orders a Pernod.'

They both began to laugh and soon a third joined in, for the bird seemed to bear no malice.

'It's been a useful lesson for him,' said Monsieur Langelin. 'I expect they made him warmly welcome at Mother Dutilleul's place. It's different here and he's soon discovered the difference between the "Eldorado" and the Green House.'

The bird had stopped scratching and preening himself. He now turned and twisted his head, as if to make sure that he had not broken his neck, and then he fixed the man and the boy with a glittering eye.

'We going to have a bite to eat?' he asked as though it were the most natural thing in the world.

'Oh, no!' groaned Monsieur Langelin. 'I hope he doesn't expect caviare and foie gras. What on earth does that sort of bird eat anyway? You can't feed him like a canary.'

'I don't know,' Cady said. 'Perhaps you give him green stuff and corn. At a pinch he could have bread soaked in milk. If he's really hungry, he'll eat whatever we give him.'

'You cut the bread. I'll heat a couple of soup cubes in the saucepan. Then we'll all have dinner.'

They kept a careful eye on their guest as they swallowed their first mouthfuls. On the surgery table Igor happily pecked at his food, sending bread crumbs and drops of milk flying in all directions. It was then that they heard a whining at the door.

Monsieur Langelin sighed wearily. 'Now we've got the other one. Really, you do seem to attract all the scroungers.'

'I'll let him have the crust off my bread,' Cady pleaded for Pignouf.

'All right. Let him in.'

The dog barked his thanks and then sprawled on the camp-bed as if he owned it. Igor looked up from his dinner.

'Hullo, Fido!' he called in a friendly fashion. 'You going to have a bite to eat, or are you going to give us a song?'

From Pignouf's throat there came an ear-splitting howl. Monsieur Langelin looked up imploringly.

'If both of them join in the conversation,' he said, 'we shan't be able to hear ourselves speak.'

Cady laughed and laughed; he was beginning to think the Green House really sheltered an invisible guest. The three old witches from the gipsies' encampment lit their lamp here, not from superstition, but to warm their old hearts in front of the tiny red flame which burned so straight in the darkness.

Every so often he glanced towards the end of the room.

'What are you looking for?' Monsieur Langelin asked him.

'Nothing,' Cady muttered.

'There's nothing there, anyway. Only the two of us, the talking bird and this skinny hound which is so heartlessly ill-treated. Isn't that enough?'

Cady looked him full in the eyes.

'You're the parish priest of the shanty-town.'

Monsieur Langelin's face betrayed nothing.

'It took you a long time to guess that, didn't it? But don't go telling everyone or the Mangler will throw me to the lions.'

Cady strove for some time to find the right words to establish their alliance.

'I like you a lot, you know.'

Calmly the Guardian Angel swallowed a mouthful of soup and put down his spoon.

'I know,' he said in the same tone of voice. 'You've no need to tell me. But in Bois-Bréau there's no room for soft-heartedness so long as these bird-slayers threaten our living quarters.'

A jerk of his thumb took in the dark kingdom of the Mangler beyond their walls. Cady was amazed.

'You don't talk like a priest,' he said.

'Do you think Jesus wore kid gloves to deal with thieves and hypocrites? The Apostles did not tell the whole story.'

Cady thought about this for a minute. The myna had finished his snack and was now strutting up and down the table, beak poised, waiting for a suitable opening in the conversation.

'We having one for the road?' he said at last. 'But make it a quick one. The forecast says we'll get frost in the Morvan.'

'Sit down and shut up,' the Guardian Angel said roughly to him. 'Listen to him, you can't take him anywhere, as soon as he has a full belly he starts to kick up a row.'

With one hop, Igor was on Cady's left shoulder. There he kept quiet, his head tucked under his wing.

'The best thing we can do,' Monsieur Langelin said, after he had thought about it for a while, 'is to hide him with someone we can trust. What about the Casbah? The Mangler will never dare cross the Wadi Radam.'

'But where would he be better off than here?' Cady replied.

They looked at the wretched bundle of feathers which had brought such trouble and strife to the shanty-town and the noble forest which lay at its doorstep. His charitable work, however, had not deprived the Guardian Angel of a certain blunt plain speaking.

'Why are those crooks so determined to get him?'

'That's our business,' Cady answered, 'not yours!'

'You're just kids.'

'There are plenty of things in life that are not the concern of a holy man.'

Monsieur Langelin's temper rose.

'You deserve a good clout!'

'I've had my share for today already,' Cady sighed as he gingerly felt the bump on his nose.

7

Little Rats

WELL BEFORE two, a large crowd of children flowed towards the door of the school carrying a remarkable collection of old rubbish, rotting rags and even a bale of straw. Monsieur Langelin stacked it all in the corner of the room in which the stove was blazing merrily, giving off sparks and puffs of sickening smoke.

'We'll have lessons for the first hour,' their Guardian Angel told his flock when the room had warmed up. 'And then we'll organise some games for the rest of the afternoon.'

'What about tea?' a number of anxious voices enquired.

'Madame Meunier will be bringing us some bread and milk in a minute. Now be good and don't make too much noise—there's someone asleep behind the desk.'

It was the myna. Cady had built him a comfortable nest from an old piece of blanket placed in the bottom of a deep cardboard box. If the bird suddenly decided to talk, all that was needed to silence him was for someone to replace the lid.

The older children had not returned and the benches at the back of the class remained empty. Having topped up the stove, Cady vanished discreetly. This caused Monsieur Langelin some anxiety.

'Whatever can they be doing out of doors in this horrible weather? Have you seen them?'

'They've got their clubs and sticks with nails in them again,' Pimpin Léonard told him. 'The Mangler and all his gang have just come back to the village. We're keeping an eye on them! For the time being they've got their heads together in the canteen. If they try to pull another hut down, Sandra's going to give the alarm and we will all have a go at them. We're armed, you know. Look. . . . '

Monsieur Langelin saw a waving forest of clubs and pokers. Serafina Torrente twirled a rusty bicycle chain.

'Put that away at once and fold your arms. We'll start with a writing lesson. Now who wants to go up to the blackboard?'

He looked behind him. Igor was still asleep, his sleek head half hidden under a fluff of feathers.

Outside, the fog had at last cleared, but it was a grey and lowering sky which closed over the outskirts of the city. To camouflage her intentions from the invading force ensconced in the canteen, Sandra had arranged a game of football in the Champs-Elysées, halfway between the 'Eldorado' and the Green House. She refereed while the Spaniards and the Portuguese enthusiastically kicked a punctured football about. There was a squelching sound as it bounced against the houses fronting the street.

'Take it easy!' she said. 'Don't send it through Fatty's windows. Let them knock back their rot-gut in peace!'

Cady was strolling down the alley where the Rouviers lived, the Boubarka brothers at his side. Every so often one of them would slip off to the corner of the street to spy at the windows of the canteen in which the lights had already been switched on.

'Still nothing,' Simbad said when he came back. 'I wonder who those villains are planning to go for.'

'Filochard and the Dormouse left their red lorry behind,' Ali observed to him. 'So it doesn't look as though they're going to evict anyone.'

'If you ask me,' Cady said, 'I'll bet they're going

hunting again. And that'll be another chance for us to make them look like a bunch of idiots.'

'Steady on,' Simbad retorted. 'The Mangler wasn't born yesterday. Do you honestly think they're going to all this fuss over a rotten bird that can't fly a hundred yards without landing four or five times? Come off it!'

'Igor can talk,' Cady said.

'Like a parrot. But I've never heard him telling the world that the scrap-men of Bois-Bréau are thieves and murderers.'

'As far as they are concerned the scraps of nonsense he talks are just as compromising. That's why they're scared of him.'

The first to emerge were Old Fred and the Crocodile, with King Kong and Bouboule. They flexed their muscles affectedly as they swaggered up the Champs-Elysées, intercepted the football, and scored a goal for the Portuguese just to show what nice fellows they were. Sandra gave a long-drawn whistle, not in her capacity as referee, but to warn the gipsies lurking at the upper end of the village.

At once Zalko and his friends popped out of the undergrowth round their encampment, and followed the men. They kept their distance, but scorned concealment: in fact they behaved rather as if they had been keeping up with the clowns and acrobats when a circus parades through the streets of a town.

'We don't need you around!' the Crocodile threatened them.

'We've heard you are in a spot of bother over a bird,' little Mischa Bauer replied. 'Except for Madame Gomez' hens, we haven't a single one in our place, so we thought we'd like to see the one you were looking for.'

'We shan't touch your hens,' said Old Fred. 'We're just doing something about extending the shanty-town.'

110

They could not shake off the grinning children who seemed to have nothing better to do than follow them about, muttering secret instructions among themselves, suddenly disappearing into the bushes only to reappear again far ahead as if they were scouting out the land for them. No threat seemed to deter them. King Kong so lost patience with little Zédé, who was almost treading on his heels, that he picked up a clod of earth and flung it in his face. At once a volley of stones whistled about his ears.

'Keep your tempers,' the Crocodile advised his friends. 'We'll settle with them tomorrow or the day after. For the time being the Mangler wants no trouble with those snotty-nosed brats.'

Then, below them, out came the second group comprising Filochard and the Dormouse, accompanied by two real toughs, Marius and Bébé-Cadum. They passed in front of the alley where the Rouviers lived and made straight for the Wadi Radam, smoking like a geyser in the frosty air.

'Four beauties!' Ali grinned. 'Sandra says they wash in lubricating-oil. Let's watch and see where they're going to hunt the little bird.'

When they reached the gaping mouth of the Wadi, the men cut away to their left, between the Casbah and the Portuguese part of the village.

'Manoel's on guard with the Torres brothers and little Pepe,' Simbad said, 'so we've nothing to worry about there. They could sneak through to the cemetery wall and take the Casbah in the rear, but if they do they'll come unstuck. Twelve of our men are out of work, including Mourab's dad, and they'll be glad of the chance of taking it out on those idiots.'

'Third lot coming out!' Cady called. He had been watching the door of the 'Eldorado'.

'Big Jules and one of the foundry-workers,' said Ali.
'The one they call Arsène.'

'He looks properly cheesed,' Simbad observed. 'Wonder
where his mate is?'

'Philippon is the one who got me these,' Cady admitted
as he pointed to his boots. 'If there's one of the Mangler's
gang who's decent, it's him. I'm glad he's not there.'

The squad turned sharp right and disappeared down an
alley leading to the main road.

'It's the Italians' turn this time,' Simbad piped up.
'Beppo and his mates are on watch in an empty house. If
the demolition-men go into action again, he'll whistle
three times to warn Sandra.'

It had become bitterly cold. Scattered snow-flakes
fluttered in the air and the sky grew darker and more
overcast. The lights in the windows of the 'Eldorado'
shone more brightly on the main street where the inter-
national between Spain and Portugal was still being
stubbornly fought out. Then the ball burst in two and the
shapeless bits fell on the scrum of players like a dying
bird.

For a fourth time the door of the canteen opened and
there stood the Mangler, his green hat pulled down over
his eyes. Behind him stood Felletin the Cosh, his weapon
swinging negligently from his wrist, and the biggest thug
in Bois-Bréau, Battling Flagada, muffled to the ears in his
magnificent red sweater.

'I hope the parade's over,' Cady said. 'I expect they've
left Théo and Spud to look after the bar.'

This last group crossed the street and plunged into the
winding alley that led up from the corner of Bofano's
grocery. The housewives standing in front of the shop
greeted them in several languages and with insulting
gestures which said much for the popularity of the
gentlemen concerned.

112

'They like us less and less,' the Mangler chuckled as he went by. 'It looks as though Old Father Kovacovici has been pressing them too hard. Let them wait and see. They're ever so impatient for Father Christmas, but they'll find he's going to drop an eviction order down their chimneys—and then I'll get rid of the whole lousy lot of them!'

A little further on, they came across a group of hockey-players battling over a round stone with the roughest of sticks. The game came to a sudden stop when they appeared. The Mangler immediately recognised the cheeky little boy whom he had clouted in the Green House.

'You haven't seen that bird again, have you?' he said in a sugary voice, as if the question were not of the slightest importance.

'There's one at the end of the alley,' Cady answered. 'He's half frozen, but there's still some life in him. If you take him into Fatty's bar and give him a Pernod, maybe he'll find his tongue again.'

The Mangler and his men turned sharply to stare in the direction to which Cady had pointed. Just outside the very last hovel lay a black bird. Now and again he gave a series of stiff little hops and then slowly collapsed with a despairing trill.

'Give me your cosh,' the Mangler hissed at Felletin. 'You two keep behind me, and don't make a sound. We've got him this time!'

They tiptoed forward, and when they were a few yards from the target, the Mangler slowly raised his arm and took careful aim. Suddenly the bird sat up. A flicker of life returned and it flew clumsily over the roof squawking in alarm. The cosh whistled through the empty air.

'Get round behind that shack and hurry!' the Mangler yelled. 'I'll wait behind this wall. Whatever happens he can't get far!'

Weak with laughter, the hockey-players slipped silently into the mouth of an alleyway. Cady whistled three notes and immediately Mimile Rouvier's face appeared in the window of a tumbledown shack.

'The coast's clear,' Simbad hissed at him. 'They're all behind the Léonards' place . . . Have you got your stuff?'

Out came the small boy reeling twenty yards of string round the corpse of a bird.

'Cut along to the Portuguese,' Cady told him. 'Take the long way round the main street. Manoel's got a splendid place all ready for you to put out your lure. While you're doing that, we'll pick those lunatics up again and drive them towards you. Don't make your crow jump too high: he looked as though he was having them on.'

Mimile met his big sister on the corner by Bofano's grocery. The ball being in the state it was, Sandra had just blown an early full time and sent the players slinking silently home through the narrow alleys of the shanty-town.

'Don't get caught,' she told her younger brother. 'The Mangler and his thugs will capture that poor old bird in the end. If they find you at the other end of the string, you'll be the one they'll use their coshes on.'

'I'll be miles away by then,' Mimile assured his sister.

The disappointed hunters stood on the edge of the Bois-Bréau to get their breath back and looked at the crumbling hovels at the end of the village. Most of them had gaping cracks in walls and roof and their occupants had draped them with old tarpaulins or tent-canvas to keep out the weather.

'The footing we put in and the planks are still sound,' the Mangler observed. 'If these folk were the slightest bit good with their hands, they could have built something nice for themselves. Five years ago, when Plastorex started building, Bois-Bréau brought us in as much rent as a twelve-storey block of flats. Now the whole thing's falling apart around us, and it's the kids who are at the bottom of it—people aren't even scared of getting beaten up now.'

'You've hit the nail on the head,' Felletin said gloomily. 'There's too many kids and they grow up too fast. What we need is a good clean sweep, a good wave of 'flu like the one we had in '57.'

The Mangler was still watching the houses. He secured his grip on his cosh.

'Where's that wretched bird gone?'

'You think it was ours all right?'

'Almost certain. It's about the same size and just as clumsy. You saw the way it flew? It was all it could manage to get over the roof.'

Then they noticed the hockey-players coming from the Spanish end of the village, whacking their stone along.

'Slipped through your fingers, has he?' Cady dropped his stick.

'Mind your own business!' the Mangler bellowed.

'There's one flapping about on the other side of the road. The Portuguese were chasing it only a moment ago. I wonder if it's the same one?'

'Just where was it?'

'Between the Torres' and the Pereiras' houses,' Simbad answered.

'You stay where you are!' Felletin shouted at them. 'If you get in our way I'll wring your necks!'

Off they went, jumping at the slightest sound as they walked from house to house along the back paths, a network of dark and narrow passageways filled with greasy paper and filth. On their approach, frightened figures vanished as smartly as rabbits down their holes. But the fair-haired boy had not been lying, and they could hear in the distance the shrill cries of the Portuguese children in pursuit of something.

115

The three men came out into a muddy little square, where two alleys running through that part of the village crossed. Their arrival scared off a group of children whose faces were blue with cold. There was the black bird at the corner of a windowless shack, the invisible thread pulling it along by the wall. It moved in a series of short bounds, four or five yards at a time, with wings dragging on the ground and head jerking convulsively. The dusk helped the illusion, as did the blind enthusiasm of men set on the capture of so miserable an object.

'He's half dead,' Battling Flagada whispered. 'He'll never be able to fly.'

'Keep clear, you clumsy lout!' the Mangler retorted angrily. 'Dead he may be, but one look at your ugly mug would be enough to send him flying to the other side of Paris.'

'Don't you think his neck's twisted in a funny way?' Felletin whispered, suddenly suspicious.

'Come on!' the Mangler bellowed.

They flung themselves forward. The bird escaped, hedge-hopping like a partridge, and vanished round the corner of the house. Just as it was about to take off, the Mangler got it and brought it down with a tremendous blow of his cosh.

'If he says another word after that, you can call me Queen of the May!'

'Is this really the one?' Felletin asked. 'The bird you were talking about this morning was supposed to have a red beak—well, this one's black as pitch.'

The Mangler picked the bird up by its wing: its beak was black.

'I may not have seen properly. It was dark in that school.'

Then, to his amazement, he noticed the string trailing on the ground, but at that very instant the bird leaped from his hand and disappeared behind a wall, once more tugged by more than human strength. The three of them dashed off in pursuit and as they came round the house ran full tilt into Filochard, the Dormouse and their toughs returning from the Casbah. The dead bird bounced along at one end of a piece of string; at the other stood the Dormouse, hauling it in hand over hand.

'I'll teach you to make a monkey of me!' yelled the Mangler. 'Here's something to be going on with!'

With that he swung a tremendous uppercut which laid the Dormouse out cold. His companions protested vigorously.

'He didn't do a thing! There was a kid playing with a bit of string. When he saw us coming he dropped it and ran. We wanted to see what was on the end of it, so the Dormouse just pulled it. That's all it was!'

The dead crow lay a little to one side, flat on its back. The toughs picked the Dormouse up and shook him like a sack of coals to wake him up. The Mangler did not bother with apologies.

'What kid was this?'

'We don't know them all,' Filochard replied. 'You can never tell the difference, they're all just as grubby.'

'Well, was he French, Italian, Spanish, Portuguese or Algerian?'

'Find out for yourself,' sighed Bébé-Cadum.

The Mangler picked up the bird reluctantly and turned it over and over as he tried to make up his mind.

'It must be the one,' he said at last. 'Don't you really think it looks like the one in the paper?'

'You've never heard of a crow talking,' Felletin the Cosh objected.

'A good trainer can make any creature you like talk —even a kipper. It's all a matter of patience.'

This raised a sycophantic titter.

'Wrap him in a rag and shove him under your coat,' the Mangler told Bébé-Cadum. 'We'll go back to the canteen. Théo can shove the whole lot on the stove and that will be that. We'll have this nightmare off our backs.'

They peered down every alleyway as they walked slowly back to the 'Eldorado'. Tiny shadows vanished as they approached and came out again once they had passed on. There was a scuffling and a sound of animal-like cries and stifled laughter.

'Little rats!' hissed the Mangler. 'Need to get rid of the lot of them. Leave it for a day or two so as to soothe their suspicions and then we'll put the screws on them again. Send the odd bulldozer down, too; that'll scare them stiff.'

They were careful to leave the canteen before the men got home from work and as they walked back towards the main road, they staggered and guffawed like men who were drunk.

The look-outs shadowed them all the way up the track, keeping well under cover and only returning when they had seen the whole gang across the road and into its stronghold. The snow still fell softly and Bois-Bréau began to look almost pretty in the white cloak which gradually covered its more ugly spots.

'It was because of those swine that my mum and dad were gassed!' Sandra confided to Cady. 'They called it getting their own back, but one night one of them climbed on our roof and blocked the stove-pipe with cotton waste. Luckily for Mimile and me, we were sleeping in the grandparents' place next door. The next morning the police investigated it, but can you imagine who they sent? A little inspector in glasses who pulled up his trousers every time he had to cross a puddle. They never found out who'd done it. But as far as I'm concerned they're all equally guilty of murder. When I was smaller they scared me, but now I've put on a bit of weight, I've got over that.

I wouldn't leave Bois-Bréau, not if you said I could have a year's holiday in the Bahamas, I want to see them brought down one by one, and then collared by a whole gang of fuzz. They're on the down-grade now. I shan't forget that crow-hunt, or the way little Mimile pulled the string. But you know I thought they'd be tougher than that.'

'They are,' said Cady, 'but only at their own game, pinching stuff on moonless nights, pulling down shacks made of cardboard and beating up people who can't hit back . . . '

8

The Rescue of the
Good Thief

THE GROUP scattered at the top of the Champs-Elysées.
The gipsies grinned goodbye and walked up the hill to
their camp: Sandra walked home with Mimile and the
Boubarka brothers, and Cady was left alone as the snow
fell slowly from the overcast sky. There was a glimmer of
golden light from the windows of the Green House, so he
tapped shyly at the door. The Guardian Angel opened it
slowly and peered cautiously out.

'I was waiting until you came back. Your dinner's on
the stove in the surgery—meat hash and vegetables—our
kind fairy got it ready, and all you have to do is heat it up
again. Don't burn the darned place down and don't take
advantage of our hospitality. The only creature allowed in
is the dog—nobody and nothing else.'

Cady leaped to the door and gave a short sharp whistle.
Pignouf was there at once, with his tousled coat and his
whole hind-quarters wagging. Monsieur Langelin dared
not raise his right hand in blessing over boy and dog. His
passage through the hell of the shanty-towns had made
him slowly lose the habit of such gestures.

'How's the bird?' Cady asked.

'He's behaved perfectly all the afternoon. You'd think
his binge in the "Eldorado" had made him lose his voice.'

Cady looked up to the roof and whistled three notes on

a rising scale. Down came the demon, who banked gracefully and settled on the hand held out to him.

'Well, Charlie, stopped saying hullo to your old pal?'

'You've got your name in the papers, you have,' Cady said.

Nervously the Guardian Angel slipped his coat on and vanished into the darkness to escape this overpowering guest. Cady locked the door behind him and warmed up the meal, which he ate at once. The excitement of the afternoon had given him an appetite, but all the same he did not forget the bird and the dog. He scarcely heard the muffled tread of the men coming home from work. Then, his leisurely meal over, Igor jumped from the table on to Cady's shoulder.

Cady carried him to the master's desk, popped him into his carton and closed the lid to get a little peace at last. Pignouf was already sprawled on the camp-bed, warming the blankets and keeping an ear cocked for the slightest sound outside. Soft footfalls had been prowling round the Green House for the past few minutes.

Without a thought for the Guardian Angel's instructions, Cady opened the door and his friends came shyly in out of the darkness. It was a proper delegation, comprising the Boubarkas, Zalko and his brother, the Torres and the Garcias, Beppo Torrente and his little sister Serafina, César Mahmadou and a pair of young Africans, Pimpin Léonard and Mimile Rouvier, and the hefty brown-haired girl to whom the weaklings ran for protection.

'We wanted to find out just what's stirred up the Mangler and his villains,' she said.

'A talking bird,' Cady retorted drily.

'It's not just that. They started to get scared that night when the grey lorry broke down by the railway-bridge. That was the first time they've ever really fought among themselves, and some of them were nearly murdered. But

121

they were left with one score to settle and now they've done just that. When Zalko came off watch he found one of them lying in the bushes on the bank by the cross-roads. We've brought the body back to you.'

They stood aside, and there lying on the snowy ground was a man, his face a mask of blood. Cady had a job to recognise the kind-hearted villain, Philippon.

'We aren't as bad as all that,' Sandra finished up. 'If we'd left him lying there in the snow, he'd have been a goner by morning.'

Cady opened the door wider.

'Put him on the camp-bed. Then lock and bolt the door, while I try to bring him round with what's in the place.'

'I'll stay outside with Loulou and keep guard,' Zalko said. 'If you hear me whistle, turn out the lights and don't make a sound.'

The dog gave up its seat to the injured man. After they had been dabbing it with antiseptic for a minute or two, Philippon reluctantly opened an eye—the other was so badly swollen that they could not see it for purple bruises. Cady had, however, succeeded in cleaning up his face, stopping the bleeding from the cuts in his bristly hide and bandaging a right ear swollen to twice its normal size.

'The Mangler said he'd have his skin,' he muttered as he removed a compress, 'but he's only lost a bit of it here and there.'

Philippon's swollen lips tried to grin.

'I fought back,' he murmured. 'It was a job for them to put me down, although they were six to one.'

'Any bones broken?'

He slowly moved his arms and legs.

'Just bruises, but I feel as though a steam-roller's run over me. It's my back which hurts most.'

'Try and sit up if you can.'

He did not succeed. Cady turned him over on his

stomach, rolled his own sleeves up, and slid his hand between Philippon's shirt and his skin. The man groaned. It was as though a red-hot iron went up and down his backbone. After a moment, the burning heat steadied at one particular place and then suddenly it spread and brought almost complete relief. Cady made him lean first on one elbow, then on the other, first move his left leg, then his right, and all the while his massaging fingers kept up their pressure.

'The second and third lumbar vertebrae are strained,' he said at last. 'If I was a works' doctor, I'd send you home with a splendid medical certificate. You'd be off work for a week. You must have fallen from quite a height, and pretty hard, with nothing to break your fall.'

'It was getting over the fence,' Philippon admitted. 'They thought they'd half killed me, so they shoved me in the cellar under the offices. While they were away I managed to break out, smash down two or three doors and escape to the far side of the yard over by the Plastorex site. I had just enough strength to crawl as far as the road and over the intersection. The only place I could hide was somewhere in the shanty-town, so it ended with me falling into the bushes.'

Cady helped him to turn over so that he was lying on his back.

'It doesn't hurt anywhere now,' he said in astonishment. 'So it's true what they say on the building-sites?'

'If Old Fred and his lads had chucked you in the hydraulic press, I wouldn't have been able to do anything for you. Why did they beat you up?'

'Because of your boots. They came from our place. The trouble is they aren't the only ones trotting round the village. There's an odd pair of the same brand, one on the right foot and one on the left of those two lads over there.

123

But I could swear that that pair never came out of the shed, and I've got the key.'

The Boubarka brothers bent down in astonishment. The left boot of the one and the right boot of the other each carried a white vulture impressed into the top of the leg.

'Those are the wellingtons they pinched from me the first time I turned up,' Cady announced.

'Well, the Mangler spotted them, this morning, here in this very room, when he was looking for the bird.'

Ali and Simbad remembered at once how the Scrap-metal King had been down on all fours by their bench searching for the bird from the grey lorry. The sight of this other white bird with its wings spread had made him just as anxious.

'Where did they come from?' Philippon insisted.

Cady thought hard.

'It all goes back to October,' he said at last. 'I was still at Moulin-Noir in those days. One morning some mates of mine told me there was a foreign lorry parked on the corner by the main road. The driver was having a drink in the shanty-town bar, fifty yards up the road. We wasted no time. The older ones climbed aboard and started to chuck the load over the tail board. Wellingtons, that was all. They were packed in huge containers double-stacked right to the back. We beat it when we saw the driver coming back, but twenty or so of us had managed to get a free pair of boots.'

Philippon winked his one good eye.

'What about the rest of the load?'

'There was nothing but boots.'

'Well, they finished up in the holds of the pirates of Bois-Bréau. They'll snap up anything that's any use, even if it's bulky and not worth very much. I expect you're beginning to realise that there'd been a different load on that Italian lorry before it stopped at Moulin-Noir.'

124

'What?'

'Something a good deal more expensive than rubber boots, and something you can quite easily take the manufacturers' name off—a couple of hundred refrigerators made by a firm in Turin.'

'Where were they unloaded?' Cady asked.

'With the Mangler's partner. He's the one who gets rid of the expensive stuff on the side, things like washing-machines, electric-cookers, 'fridges, TV sets, transistors and that sort of thing. It's an easy job for him, he owns a chain of thirty shops throughout France, trading under a highly respectable name. He dresses well, he keeps his mouth shut, and he never shows his face in the Mangler's place. But you only have to open that door, and there it is right in front of you on the other side of the road, a high wall a hundred and fifty yards long, and him sitting snug behind it.'

'Demagny's Warehouses!' Sandra exclaimed.

Exhausted by all he had said, Philippon sank back. Slowly his one good eye, his left, closed and he said no more. In the surgery cupboard, behind the rolls of bandages, Cady discovered a bottle bearing the red label —*Only to be taken on doctor's orders*. He uncorked it and sniffed the smooth smell of Kirsch. The injured man swallowed half the liqueur in one gulp. As he went back to sleep again he said in tones of satisfaction:

'That was a drop of the real stuff!'

'You just go off to sleep,' Sandra told him. 'You're quite safe here. Nobody's going to break the door down. Tomorrow morning we'll smuggle you out of the shanty-town under the noses of Fatty and the Mangler. Once you're clear, get moving and head for Paris, it's quite close. So long as you don't hang around here, you needn't worry. In fact, you ought to thank the old Mangler for trying to get rid of you. The day the fuzz come to Bois-Bréau, I hope you'll be miles away.'

She helped Cady tuck him in, and then they all withdrew to the other end of the room. The noise had wakened Igor, who whistled, and chirruped, and expressed his displeasure in his own way from inside his box.

'He's a bird who must have company,' Cady observed. 'Shall I let him out for a minute or two? If he makes a fuss we can always shut him up again for the rest of the night.'

He lifted the lid. Out shot Igor like a Jack-in-the-box, perched on his master's shoulder and chattered away like an old woman.

'Sit still and shut up!' Cady spoke harshly to him. 'Any trouble out of you and we'll chuck a bucket of water over you and put you back to bed!'

The threat sank in. Igor hunched his wings crossly and did not breathe another word. Cady lifted him off and put him on the end of the master's desk. He was pleased to be so high up in the world and perched there at the ready, his beak pointing outwards. His little white-rimmed eyes stared first at one of the children, then at another. Philippon had raised a tiny corner of the veil of mystery surrounding the myna, and very gradually they were beginning to understand.

'I managed to get a look at grand-dad's paper,' Sandra said. 'Vi and Rosie weren't making things up this morning when they told us what they heard through the window of the "Eldorado". It's quite true that Igor's got his picture on the front page, I saw it, and there's a long bit about the grey lorry we saw the other night. That's the reason why the Mangler came raging down here in the afternoon with all his thugs and searched the village from top to bottom. Igor's a damning piece of evidence against him, and he talks! He could bring the fuzz down in five minutes, as sure as if he was a long-range burglar-alarm!'

Simbad shrugged.

'All because of his yarns?'

'No. Simply because he's here and not somewhere else. Suppose the fuzz did find him in Bois-Bréau. The first thing they'd do would be to search the area; and they'd start with the most suspicious place in it—the Mangler's scrap-yard—and sooner or later that would send them knocking at the gates of Demagny's Warehouses. There've been two bits of luck which may bring them here. In the first place the grey lorry broke down a couple of hundred yards away from the Croix-Souci cross-roads, and in the second place the myna bird took it into its head to join us and was good enough to follow us back to the shanty-town. There you are!'

'What did the paper say about the lorry?' Beppo asked.

'It was coming back from Germany with a valuable load on board. They reckon it was worth several million francs. Electronic equipment, tape-recorders, colour TV-sets ... It was stolen early in the afternoon from a transport café by the Porte d'Ivry, Mother Dutilleul's Place. It was a regular pull-up for the crew, which shows they must have had their eye on them for some time.

'The driver, Gaston Perrot, and his young mate, Charlie Rouvet, reported it to the nearest police-station. But by then it was too late. If you know your route beforehand, you can shift a big lorry pretty quick, even if you've got to get it right across Paris from south to north. All their gear was in the cab, and that included Charlie's mascot, a tame myna bird he took everywhere with him—our old friend Igor!'

The myna came in on cue.

'Wotcher, mates! If you feel like a drink, we'll stop at Montelimar ... '

'Shut up, or back in your box you go!' Cady warned him and got up from his bench.

Igor gave way and hid his head under his left wing.

'As you might expect,' Sandra went on, 'the papers took up the story, and of course they gave the kidnapped bird star-billing, because it could put the police on the scent while it was still warm. But poor old Charlie couldn't care less about the lorry or the thieves. He's offering a reward of five hundred francs to the kind soul who brings his old pal back safe and sound ... Now you can see why the scrap-men fought like tigers that night. First of all they unloaded the lorry into one of the warehouses at Demagny's, then the Dormouse got in to drive it off and leave it some six or seven miles from Bois-Bréau, only to have a break-down just by the railway-bridge. Filochard tried to get it to go, but couldn't, so then they were in a jam! They couldn't leave it lying almost on the Mangler's doorstep, for once it was found their hideout would be discovered. If they towed it away and left it in the next parish it would mean a long and risky job. The theft was hours old and the police had issued a description of the lorry by then and given its registration number. The only way out was to take it straight back to the yard and either repaint it or dismantle it altogether. After the Mangler had stepped in, this is what they decided to do. Meantime Charlie's myna had started to spin his yarns to us and made his home in the Green House. Whatever the gang's done with the grey lorry, it doesn't matter. But Igor's just slipped through their fingers for the second time, and this bunch of crooks is in real danger!'

She paused, peering uncertainly at her friends.

'And now, what ought we to do?'

The first thing they considered was the incriminating evidence itself, the myna sitting like a judge over them.

'It's plain as a pikestaff,' César Mahmadou declared. 'We just tie a label to his leg with the Mangler's name and address on it and let him go. Sooner or later he's bound to land up in a police-station and spill the beans to the fuzz. Then they'll be round here before you know what.'

The others roared with laughter.

'That's the nicest way of fixing those swine,' Sandra agreed. 'But I'd be scared in case Igor finished up in the ditch. Once he's dead, he's no good to anyone.'

Beppo Torrente considered the problem.

'Five hundred francs! Just think of that,' he said, puffing out his cheeks. 'That's money! Just think what you could buy with that!'

'Charlie's never going to guess where his bird is,' Simbad objected. 'We'll have to write to him. Then he's bound to bring the fuzz to collar the gang.'

There was something about the way he said this which showed that the prospect did not entirely please him. Cady was amused by his perplexity.

'That's not really what you want?'

'We'd lose the whole point of it,' Sandra answered. 'If you ask me, the Mangler and his thugs deserve a different sort of punishment, something spectacular, where we can all join in like we did this afternoon. Suppose, for instance, we were to chuck them into the Wadi Radam one by one. That would be the best way of clearing them off our bit of land. And if one of them was lucky enough to come out alive, he'd never be able to wash off the stink for the rest of his days.'

Igor joined their laughter and then his red beak swung sharply round to the far end of the room. A key turned softly in the lock. The older children scampered over to the door to defend their patient, but it was only a false alarm. In came the three witches from the gipsies' encampment, muffled in their brightly-coloured shawls and carrying the little copper lamp which sanctified their meditations.

'Off home with you!' one of them clucked angrily.

The swarthy-faced boys crept away obediently and Simbad and Beppo shooed the others out so as not to make the caretaker's task any harder. Sandra and Mimile were left by themselves with Cady, who politely stood to one side for his visitors. Igor had not shifted from his perch and his little round eye was fixed on them. Cady dreaded the sort of thing he might say, including the fatal invitation to the bar on the corner. However, the myna behaved himself, never saying a word nor even flinching when they lit their lamp on the other corner of the desk.

When they had done this the three old ladies sat down on a bench in the middle and wrapped themselves in meditation.

'Does this go on for long?' Sandra whispered.

'Five or ten minutes, seldom more. You mustn't laugh at them. I expect they're saying their prayers.'

'Who to?' Mimile asked.

'I don't know, and as far as I can see, nobody answers them. But all the same they keep on coming back and lighting their lamp.'

Sandra shrugged.

'If there is a God, he's far too far away to hear us in Bois-Bréau or answer us so as we can understand.'

'You never know,' Cady said, almost to himself. 'The Guardian Angel makes out it isn't a waste of time.'

In the corner of the surgery Philippon was still fast asleep. The dog had rolled himself into a ball under the bed and he did not stir either. The stove was going out. All was still outside, but you could imagine the snow-flakes drifting down and gradually covering the grimy soil.

The old gipsies made a furtive sign of the cross, got up at last, put out their lamp and vanished like ghosts.

Sandra took Mimile by the hand and made for the door.

130

'They gave you a funny look as they left,' she said mockingly to Cady. 'You're not going to tell me they think you're the Baby Jesus, too?'

He did not smile. He had other things to think about. As she went out, Sandra looked back from the roadside.

'One of us has got to volunteer to report these crooks,' she murmured to him. 'I hope we get rid of them before Christmas.'

'It won't be either you or me,' Cady replied. 'That's none of our business. Anyway I'm sure somebody's looking after it already, or soon will be.'

9

The New Tenants

EIGHT O'CLOCK, and Cady quietly opened the door as he heard the 2 CV come complainingly down the track. Four inches of snow muffled the ground and the flakes still fluttered down from the leaden sky. He was there before Madame Meunier got out of the car, to help her unload it. Their good fairy had brought two dozen bottles of milk and enough bread to feed a regiment.

'Sleep well?' she asked him.

'On the floor,' Cady admitted, 'and so did the dog . . . I simply had to; the hospital bed has a patient from over the way in it. Would you like to take a look at him? He came over to us last night from the enemy camp, but he was in such a state that we couldn't turn him away.'

He told her the whole story in detail. Madame Meunier leaned over the still-sleeping Philippon and stared into his battered face.

'Can't we be spared anything?' she said almost to herself. 'Must we even be forced to look after these crooks?'

There was no gentleness left in that face worn by a lifetime of self-effacing service and Cady was saddened by the thought that hatred could creep into this place of refuge. The noise of a motor-scooter made them prick up their ears.

'That's Monsieur Langelin. Let him in. He's the only person who can tell us what is to be done with this creature.'

132

Their Guardian Angel stamped his boots at the door-step, shook the snow from his oilskins and then stopped when he saw the shape lying in the gloom on the camp-bed. Madame Meunier was staring at the floor, while Cady, trying to smile, was spreading his hands in an innocent gesture.

'Our third guest . . .'

'So I see,' Monsieur Langelin sighed. 'And he didn't drop out of the clouds.'

He had half recognised the foundry-worker from Messrs Kovacovici.

'We can't keep Philippon a moment longer,' he told Madame Meunier when the boy had finished his explanations. 'The others are searching the cross-roads and the verges, and the Mangler's there too. Sooner or later they'll be back in the village again and they're sure to come to the school.'

'What should we do?'

'Bring your 2 CV as close to the door as you can and open it up at the back. We'll help him to crawl in and hide under the back seat. Cady can cover him as best he can with a blanket. Then I'll drive him over to a surgery near Colombes, where they treat injured workers.'

It was hard to wake Philippon. Then he listened in strained silence to the Guardian Angel's instructions, while Cady peered out to make sure that the coast was clear. The village still slumbered in the grey light of early morning, no light showed in the 'Eldorado', but there were figures on the main road gradually moving nearer and nearer to the track. It was the Crocodile, with his escort of four or five massive toughs, for Felletin the Cosh was already busy forcing his way through the under-growth on the edge of the gipsies' encampment.

Without wasting a second, Madame Meunier backed her 2 CV up to the door and got out.

133

'All clear,' she said, 'they're still some way away. But do get a move on!'

Clumsily Philippon crawled into the back of the car and hastily Cady draped him with a blanket and threw a few empty cardboard cartons on top. Monsieur Langelin had already slipped into the driver's seat. He was about to press the self-starter, when the Crocodile and his men came into sight at the top of the track. There they stood, shoulder to shoulder, as if to stop anyone passing.

The Guardian Angel paused. For one brief instant all three of them, for separate motives of generosity, were as deeply involved in his awful danger as Philippon. They were saved by the muffled hoot of a siren on the Plastorex site. It was the first call to the shift. At once the workers of Bois-Bréau surged from the alleyways and went stumping up the Champs-Elysées. The majority of these two or three hundred men who laboured so hard for so little pay, were resigned to their fate; but they could shake off their apathy and become terrible when their anger was aroused.

The Mangler's strong-arm men scattered on either side of the track and hastily took themselves off to avoid an encounter from which they would always emerge the losers. Monsieur Langelin drove the 2 CV up the track and passed safely through with the Portuguese in front and the Algerians behind. Madame Meunier watched the car vanish in the direction of Mareuil and then, with a sigh of relief, she went back into the school.

'That was a close thing.'

'A nice hot cup of coffee will soon put us right,' Cady said. 'I really need one. I didn't get a wink of sleep last night, what with the dog scratching and growling in its dreams, the myna waking up every other minute and ordering a drink and the bloke from the scrap-yard snoring like a pig. I was expecting those toughs to come

134

smashing in through the door at any minute. Now we can begin to breathe in Bois-Bréau.'

'What makes you think that?'

'The old Mangler's dead scared. His time's nearly up. He had his bit of bad luck last week, and ever since that evening the spanner's been put in his dirty works.'

Madame Meunier listened as she got the coffee and as she listened she grew more and more cheerful. She had sworn to stand firm in Bois-Bréau until the defeat of the villain who squeezed the poor with as little concern as if he had been drawing dividends from an investment. And here was a lad, breezing in from nowhere, without a penny to his name, calmly telling her that the grand spring-cleaning operation was on its way.

Five minutes later they were sadly undeceived when they heard a knock at the door. There were three sharp, insistent raps which sounded as though they had been made by the end of a cosh.

'Don't open it!' whispered Madame Meunier. 'I can't face that monster again.'

Cady was unconcerned.

'What do we risk? He may be rude to you, and he could quite likely clout me. We're small fry as far as he's concerned. Would you like to bet me he won't come inside? All I need do is say just one little word and the old Mangler'll be back up that road like a scalded cat.'

Madame Meunier could not stop him opening the door. There stood the Mangler with the Crocodile on one side of him and Felletin the Cosh on the other. Although the hood of his duffle-coat was up, you did not think of Father Christmas when you looked at the red-nosed scrap-merchant, while his lieutenants appeared positively devilish.

'I never realised you ran this school of yours like a cut-throat joint,' he said smoothly. 'There's blood on your doorstep. Come from a stray dog?'

They had swept away the snow at the very spot where the gipsies had set Philippon down a few hours before. Here and there spots of red could be seen, leading up to the Green House. Cady denied nothing and still won his bet.

'That comes from your foundry-man, but he's swallowed half a flask of Kirsch and that put him on his feet again.'

Beneath his hood the Mangler went pale.

'Where is he?'

'Honestly, I don't know. If he's stark bonkers he's lying up somewhere in the hope that you'll forget all about him. If he's any thought for his skin, he's made for the nearest first-aid post and that's the one at Mareuil. As it's built on to the police-station, he's only got to go through one door from one to the other. And I'm sure he's not bonkers, and I'm sure the Kirsch has sharpened his wits as well.'

The Mangler stepped forward and stood in the doorway.

'He's here!'

'I had a little bet with Madame Meunier that you wouldn't come in,' Cady said as he backed away. 'But all right, you can walk round the shack if you like, I shall only lose half my bet.'

The three crooks were nonplussed by his confidence.

'Why?' asked the Mangler.

'I've got a surprise for you at the other end of the room. Like to bet on that too?'

'He's putting it on,' the Crocodile sneered. 'That nurse is scared stiff.'

But the boy stood there grinning from under his clumsily-trimmed fair hair. The Mangler hesitated: he dared not take the one step which might have shortened the life of the myna bird. Cady had brought him into play just as one brings forward a piece in chess to make one's opponent commit an error. And the morale of Cady's opponent was very low. The three men just stared at the red spots on the snow and then strode away towards the main road.

'Those cats aren't scalded,' Madame Meunier said between laughter and tears.

'They've had their lot,' Cady told her confidently. 'Here and now Bois-Bréau is melting from their grasp like a handful of snow. Would you like to make another bet?'

'No!' she said in alarm.

The coffee had grown cold by this time, and they had to heat it up again in the saucepan. As Madame Meunier sipped hers, she stared at Cady through half-closed eyes. The boy was hard to understand.

'How old are you?'

'I've already told you—just over thirteen.'

'You don't look more than twelve.'

'I'd soon grow if I had three square meals a day.'

The diet of Bois-Bréau had not fattened his cheeks, but Madame Meunier could feel him bursting with happiness and energy. He answered questions readily, but she could not pin him down. Nothing mattered to him but the present, the warmth of the strong coffee which he was drinking with a friend and accomplice. She tried again with her questions.

'Have you really never had any family at all?'

'Never.'

All he could remember was the tired old lady, more than a little mad and physically weak, who was able to do good in her quiet way and without asking for anything special for herself, but who could have lived nowhere but among the dregs of society.

'My home is the shanty-town. I don't know any other place. The Mangler doesn't scare me. He's got too much money already. He may be greedy and he may be cruel, but he doesn't come anywhere near the bosses in Nanterre or Bobigny; they're jackals who fight you for the right to sleep under a scrap of canvas or hunt through the dustbins. That's where the difference is. The Scrap-metal King will fall faster because he's got far more to lose. He's tried to round off his pile with the ten acres of Bois-Bréau and in the end all they'll bring him is ten years inside.'

An hour later Monsieur Langelin drove back in the 2 CV. His cheerful smile at once reassured Madame Meunier and Cady who had just finished getting the room ready for the morning lessons.

'The nuns will only keep him there for a day or two and then they'll send him on to hospital. That face of his is too much for them, it's been smashed to pulp. But he's out of here and that's the main thing.'

It occurred to Cady then that this could prove another way of getting information to the police. Had Igor himself appeared on television, it could have hardly speeded matters any faster. The myna had, in fact, been let out and as he flew from one beam to another up in the roof he gave a prolonged whistle to clear his throat, and then began to call rudely down to his protectors.

The children from the village arrived in small groups, each well muffled up and bearing a handful of twigs or a bit of old wood to go on the stove. In another five minutes Cady had slipped quietly away without a word, the Guardian Angel's blue oilskin wrapped round him to his ankles.

The older children had been turned out of doors into the village. Their vigilance was dangerously relaxed, for now they played in the snow which had transformed Bois-Bréau. The whole village breathed an air of respite which it had never known before.

Cady caught up with Sandra in the Italian part of the

village, at the end of the alley where he had so often kept watch. Hidden among the snow-laden bushes, she was looking at a point beyond the bank. Drifting snow-flakes hid the road, but you could still see the wall on the far side and the massive iron gates of Demagny's Warehouses.

'I wonder if the thieves have set off the alarm signal?'

'They may have,' Cady answered. 'But that doesn't mean they're going to do a sudden bunk. The fact that they've got away with it for so long has made them stupid. And it must be quite a wrench to leave the loot behind.'

Sandra changed the subject abruptly.

'Philippon got clean away then?'

'In the back of the 2 CV. But only just: the Mangler's search-party was all round the Green House.'

'Will he have the sense to go to the police?'

'I shouldn't think so. I expect he thinks they'll put him inside with the rest of the gang as an accessory.'

'I'm getting desperate,' Sandra said. 'We've got enough on them to have them arrested in no time; all we've got to do is pull the string. Why are we waiting?'

Cady shook his head.

'You've never had anything to do with the fuzz, have you? Let them do their own dirty work; we'll keep right out of it. All they need to do is wander round Demagny's Warehouses and the Mangler's scrap-yard; and then if they don't see what's going on they must be blind.'

Slowly they walked down towards the Champs-Elysées, peering up each alley they passed. Everywhere blackened stove-pipes poked through the roofs and poured out clouds of stinking yellow smoke. It made Sandra anxious.

'There must be about five or six fires every winter, and they're always up the same end of the village, where the Portuguese and Spaniards hang out. Six months behind with the rent they are. By the time the fire-brigade from Mareuil gets on the scene, the fire's generally out. But a

139

few houses have been burned to the ground and the families in them have been forced to sleep in the open. I suppose it's all part of the Mangler's murder campaign. We'll have to ask the others to keep their eyes open.'

Opposite the canteen, Beppo Torrente was directing a team of sculptors to construct a snowman in the shape of Fat Théo. All the essentials were there: the round ball of a head, the great swollen belly and the arms sticking out like a pair of hams. To avoid any mistake, Serafina had crowned the creature with a red and green checked piece of rag, which was a reasonable attempt at the dishonour- able gentleman's cap. As the landlord of the 'Eldorado' watched this through his windows, his eyes nearly popped out of his head. Battling Flagada was sent out to demolish this insulting effigy, but was forced to retreat under a barrage of snowballs!

Promptly at ten o'clock they watched the arrival of Monsieur Chabot, one of the foremen who lived in the village. He came striding down the street with a tough- looking couple who carried suitcases and bedding. They made straight for the Estate Agent's Office, in other words the canteen. The door was opened with considerable caution to let them in and as it did so a score of eavesdroppers crouched under the windows of the bar to hear what went on.

'A couple of new recruits for Plastorex,' Monsieur Chabot was saying. 'Amédée and Hector Lambert. They'll be driving tipper-trucks on Number Four site. They couldn't get a room in Mareuil and they wanted some- where near the job. You haven't got anything that would do, have you?'

Théo scratched his head while he looked the newcomers up and down as if to guess what they were worth.

'It all depends,' he grunted. 'If it came to it, we could put them in the Poles' old shack. But it's fully furnished,

140

so it'll work out a lot dearer. On top of that, I'll need three months' rent in advance and a deposit on the furniture. I don't want any more of the bother I had last Thursday.'

Eventually they agreed a figure and the Lambert brothers produced their wallets and paid up. Fat Théo then ushered them to the bar and offered them a glass of white wine to give them a good impression of his den.

'My man will take the keys and show you where it is,' he said at last. 'You should like it: there's one big room and a small one with the stove and wash basin. The bottle of Butane gas is half-full, but you can have that for free . . . When do you start work?'

'Tomorrow morning,' Amédée replied.

'Don't forget to lock up after you, and watch out for the kids. The village is crawling with the little brats.'

Monsieur Chabot walked up to the main road on his own, while the Lambert brothers followed Battling Flagada through the maze of the shanty-town, themselves followed in the distance by a gang of children excitedly discussing the newcomers.

A little later Théo's 'man' left the bachelors' quarters and returned to the canteen through a fresh barrage of snowballs controlled by Lieutenant Pimpin Léonard. The statue of Fat Théo in the middle of the Champs-Elysées had doubled in size and the addition of all sorts of extras had made it look even more like the landlord of the 'Eldorado'.

It was not long before the Lambert brothers emerged, nor were they very surprised to find a few slim figures watching on their doorstep. As a peace-offering to these savages, the older of the two, Hector, held out a packet of biscuits which was instantly torn from his grasp. Like squirrels the children scattered, each to gulp down his share, and then, one by one, they came back with a friendlier look on their faces. Mimile Rouvier went so far as to offer to guide the newcomers to Bofano's grocery, show them the water-pipes, swathed in straw against the frost, point out the short-cuts to the main road and, as the crowning treat, take them to the sinister mouth of the Wadi Radam steaming in the icy air.

'Our main drainage . . . But mind you don't fall in or they'll have to drag you out of the Seine a good half-mile away!'

'What's on the other side?'

'That's what we call the Casbah, where the Algerians live. They're at daggers drawn with the bosses. We kids can go in whenever we like, but unless you're asked, grown-ups have to steer clear . . . And now you've seen the lot!'

From then on the Lamberts were treated as friends, and nobody, at least on the surface, appeared to give them another thought. However, Sandra and Simbad, under cover of a pretended game in the snow, followed them at a respectable distance, while Cady raced back to the school.

'I've never seen newcomers get in with Théo so fast,' Sandra was saying. 'They paid the top price and no arguing. If that sack of guts had a grain of sense in his head, he'd have been suspicious. If those two are truck-drivers, then I'm the Queen of England!'

Simbad felt the same way.

'It's all a scheme of the Mangler's to quell the rebellion before it starts. He's going to put a couple of toughs in each part of the village, a pair of ugly mugs we haven't seen around Bois-Bréau before.'

When they reached the middle of the Champs-Elysées, the Lambert brothers walked round the snowman, chuckled and then went straight into the canteen.

'What did I say?' groaned Simbad. 'They behave as if they were old customers already.'

But Sandra was pursuing her own line of thought.

142

'They are too, but not in the way you think. You çan meet their doubles in other shanty-towns, in the same disguise. They turn up as innocent as you please, get themselves taken on at the nearest building-site, have the odd drink in the canteen, pass the time of day with the women and kids, and then they quietly wander round the place until they pull in the man they're after. They're police inspectors: the worst sort of fuzz, real hard characters. Just what we need around here to put Messrs Kovacovici out of business!'

The Guardian Angel released the children earlier than usual so that they could play in the snow.

'All in all, a first-rate morning,' he said to Madame Meunier, 'and the afternoon should go just as peacefully. Since we've already got enough to give the children a substantial tea, I can do without you if you like. Why don't you take the chance to visit your poor old folk in Mareuil and Sartrouville?'

At once the good lady's face fell.

'I haven't a penny in the till. They won't be content with just a few kind words and a little medical treatment.'

Sorrowfully Monsieur Langelin opened his wallet, took out a couple of fifty-franc notes, handed one to his co-worker and then gave her the other as well, adding, with a heart-breaking sigh:

'Just my luck! I'll go round the Welfare people tonight. They dread me like the plague. Bois-Bréau has a bad reputation with the charitable organisations. I'll try to cook up a story that will soften them; after all, haven't we been living the opposite of a Christmas story for the last few days?'

Madame Meunier carefully folded the notes and jealously put them away in her bag. For a moment her eyes stared blankly at the village, and then at last she managed a thank-you.

'We've never been so short of money. If we get hold of enough bread and milk for the day tomorrow morning, I'll believe in God again.'

'He'd rather you did something about it yourself,' the Guardian Angel retorted with a mocking grin.

He watched the 2 CV go up the track and disappear amid the falling snow. Cady was there, standing beside him in the doorway. Sandra had given him an old pointed red woollen cap which he wore pulled down over his ears and which made him look like a goblin. Monsieur Langelin was ready to think he really had been changed into one when he heard what Cady had to say.

'As we're short of money for the Green House, the simplest thing would be to look for it where we know there is some. And where's that? In the pockets of those who are rolling in cash. I'll look after the collection, so long as I can have someone helping me go from door to door. What about Sandra? She's got a tongue in her head, for one. If we put the problem fairly to them, but tactfully mind you, our customers will soon see reason and we'll come home to Bois-Bréau tonight with a nice little sum for you.'

'What on earth are you talking about!' Monsieur Langelin replied. 'Here we are in the middle of a slum area. In the bend of the Seine between Moulin-Noir and the Ile-aux-Chiens you could count on the fingers of one hand the houses of anyone with real money.'

He pointed to the main road behind its curtain of snow.

'Can you tell me where there's one?'

'Bang opposite,' Cady answered calmly. 'For a start I'm going to knock on the gates of Demagny's Warehouses.'

144

IO

Dangerous Charity

THE FIRST thing they had to do was to tell the gang about the crazy scheme and to form a support group ready to come to their help, for the whole business had a ninety-per-cent chance of failure.

'If the caretaker does open the gate,' Simbad said, 'it'll only be to let a couple of guard-dogs loose on you. All you'll get will be a fall headfirst down the bank with your clothes in ribbons.'

The youngsters were delighted at the prospect of this encounter which promised to be the biggest joke of the year.

'We'll have a ring-side seat on the other side of the road,' Beppo Torrente said. 'If things go wrong, just give a whistle and we'll all come running with our sticks and catapults.'

'Whatever you do, don't do that,' Cady retorted. 'Everything will go all right, even if we don't get any cash, but on no account are you to come out of those bushes!'

The snow had virtually stopped since midday and the mass of cloud above their heads was momentarily shot with gold and now and again showed a rapidly vanishing patch of blue. The traffic was still much lighter than usual—the odd car being driven slowly and carefully, the tippers from the Plastorex site, a dozen lorries moving in convoy and then the slush-covered road was empty once more.

145

Cady bade his friends farewell and turned to his assistant.

'Let's go,' he said.

They took a short cut which brought them out behind the end of the village where the Italians lived, and then they plunged into the bushes on the bank. Sandra had made a mild attempt to make herself more presentable: she had run a comb through her brown hair and brushed off a little of the mud which clung to her jeans. Cady had put the Guardian Angel's dark blue oilskins over his patched and faded jerkin. The burly girl was not feeling very happy.

'To look at us, nobody would give us a sou at the street corner! We'd have the fuzz on our tails in a couple of seconds. But we wouldn't do any better if we turned up over there dressed to the nines. You'll see how they'll slam the door in our faces!'

'I'll just go on ringing and ringing, then,' Cady answered with an obstinate look on his face. 'When they get tired of opening it and shutting it and telling us to get the hell out of it, then maybe we'll slip in.'

'It's a lovely thing to have faith!' Sandra sighed. 'I'm all ready to trade punches in your defence, but I warn you there are limits to what I'll put up with. The third time they chuck us out, I'm going back to the village.'

They let a big lorry go by, throwing up the slush, and then side by side they crossed the road and walked up to the iron gate. Not a sound came from the old building. Demagny's Warehouses were as silent as the grave.

'Could they have cleared out?' Sandra asked.

'We'd have seen or heard them if they had. You don't shift two or three hundred tons of stuff without kicking up a bit of a row. I'm sure they're there . . . Do you want me to go in alone?'

'No! No!' Sandra protested. 'I don't let my mates down
. . .'

There was a small door in the right-hand gate. Cady
put his finger on the bell. They could dimly hear a ringing
sound in a distant building, but there was no immediate
reaction and nothing stirred behind the door.

'I told you they'd cleared out!' Sandra muttered.

Cady rang again. Two short sharp rings with a second
or so between them. This time somebody came. Slow,
dragging footsteps stopped behind the door and then the
door itself slowly opened to disclose a thickset, ginger-
haired man in a white coat. He had the build of the men
who worked in the scrap-yard, and there was a family
likeness about him despite the difference of his job and the
fact that here they probably washed themselves more
often than they did next door. A look of utter amazement
came over his face when he saw the tall girl and the
ragged boy standing there.

'First time you've come visiting! Sure you've come to
the right place?'

'We wanted to see Monsieur Demagny,' Cady announced firmly but politely.

The caretaker gave a hoot of laughter.

'He's been dead and buried for fifty years. The warehouses are an old family business that's been going for the
best part of a hundred years, and they've kept his name,
that's all. There's no such person as Demagny.'

'Then who's the boss?'

'Monsieur Alexandre. But we hardly ever see him.
He's got plenty to do elsewhere. What did you want
with him?'

'We're making a collection for our school,' Cady replied
with confidence. 'Funds are running very low and we
thought Monsieur Alexandre might like to help.'

'What school?' asked the bewildered caretaker.

147

'The one in Bois-Bréau. You can see it easily from here through the trees along the road. It's that little green building with the steep roof.'

'You've got a nerve, I must say! I didn't even know that muck-heap had a school. The whole place is a disgrace to the neighbourhood . . . Now get out! And look sharp about it, I don't want you bringing your fleas in here!'

'We'll bring you worse than that,' Sandra retorted.

He tried to shut the door, but she leant on it with both hands, pushing with all her might, and Cady slipped behind her into the robbers' lair. At first glance there was nothing unusual about it—an enormous paved forecourt, with warehouses round the sides, their sliding-doors half closed, and a long concrete ramp against which were backed huge black and yellow lorries bearing the trademark of Demagny. Khaki-clad workmen busied themselves with loading and unloading, working with the speed and industry of an ants'-nest around the rear of these massive vehicles. Sandra and Cady shot off to the right towards a two-storey building housing the rest-rooms and offices. Behind them the caretaker came charging like a rhinoceros.

'Come back!' he shouted. 'Come back! Or I'll set my dogs on you.'

They opened the nearest door and tumbled into a lavishly-furnished room in which five gentlemen in business suits were engaged in lively discussion at a table loaded with files of papers. The abrupt appearance of the intruders gave them a shock and the oldest of them clutched his heart. The youngest, a tall swarthy man with dark curly hair, rose threateningly to his feet.

'What are you doing in here?'

'We're looking for Monsieur Alexandre,' Cady answered. 'We want to tell him something of vital importance.'

148

'I'm the man you want,' the young man said as he walked towards them. 'And how did you get in?'

'Through the door,' Sandra replied. 'Your caretaker's not much of a watch-dog.'

The gentleman concerned stood in the doorway, his eyes rolling in terror. Monsieur Alexandre dismissed him with an impatient gesture and turned to the girl.

'What do you want?' he asked.

'A bit of money.'

'We could see that by the way you came into the room.'

The others nodded and smiled slavishly, in exactly the same way as the brutish scrap-men applauded the Mangler's jokes.

'What do you want money for?'

'We come from the shanty-town,' Cady explained. 'The school has run out of funds and we hope to raise something before the temperature goes down to twenty below . . . You've got plenty of money, I'm sure?'

Monsieur Alexandre raised his eyebrows and turned to his friends as if to ask them to bear witness to this piece of impertinence.

'Did you hear that? These kids from the shanty-town . . . Why, the cold drives them out of their hovels like rats from their holes.'

'It's better to give while you've got it,' Cady went bravely on. 'You never know what tomorrow will bring.'

'We hope it will bring you something nice,' Sandra added. 'Ours doesn't look too good as things are.'

'Get out or I'll send for the caretaker!' Monsieur Alexandre yelled.

Sandra was first out of the door; her hopes had fled. Cady turned, still clutching the door handle.

'Girls can't talk business,' he said quietly. 'I'm sure we men can reach some agreement. Would you give me something for a useful bit of information?'

149

'That depends: tell us what it is.'

'Two cops disguised as workers have rented a shack in Bois-Bréau this morning.'

Monsieur Alexandre did not move an eyelid.

'So what? This old firm has nothing to feel guilty about.'

'Your neighbours couldn't say as much.'

'What makes you think that?'

'They made a big mistake the other day ... You remember that grey lorry that came out of your warehouses on Thursday night? Well, it didn't get beyond the railway bridge.'

There was a moment's silence in the room. Monsieur Alexandre's bushy black eyebrows shot up.

'And then?'

'The Scrap-metal King had it towed back to his yard.'

The man shrugged his burly shoulders.

'What he does is no business of mine ... What else do you know? You'd better tell me.'

'Nothing more,' Cady admitted. 'But what I've told you is well worth two hundred francs.'

Instantly he wished that he had asked for more, for Monsieur Alexandre did not argue; he handed the money over as carelessly as if the whole question had ceased to interest him. However, his companions stared rigidly in front of them, and more than one of them changed colour.

By the pleased expression on Cady's face as he came out of the room, Sandra guessed what had happened.

'Let's go!'

They shot out of the gate, just dodging the caretaker's boot, and then Cady showed her the notes which he had extorted from Monsieur Alexandre.

'Two hundred francs!' she exclaimed. 'That means we've kept our side of the bargain. The Guardian Angel can hardly have expected as much as that.'

'The game's not over yet,' Cady announced. 'I don't see why the Mangler should be any more tight-fisted than the Warehouse King. So let's push off to the scrap-yard.'

'Not on your life!' Sandra screamed. 'It would be madness.'

'You always look on the black side of things. I'm scared, too, but the Mangler won't dare lift a finger to us. He'll soon realise that the whole village is watching from the other side of the road.'

'I'll go up to the gate with you, but that's as far as I'll go. Then I'm turning round and coming back.'

'Please yourself. But don't blame me if our mates treat you as if you'd let them down. We're on top now. Why, for the last few minutes I feel as though I've been walking on air.'

'Cady!' Sandra sighed and shook her head. 'Before you're much older, you're going to end up in the ditch . . . with six feet of earth on top of you.'

All the same she went with him, although she tried to slow the pace at which they were walking. First they crossed the wide and rutted road leading to the Plastorex site. Everywhere walls and columns were rising and the delicate arms of the cranes swung overhead. They were too far away to recognise the workers in their oilskins and safety-helmets.

'If I yell for help,' Sandra said, 'not even grand-dad will hear me. And we've nothing to defend ourselves with.'

They reached the fence round the scrap-yard, peering through the cracks in it as they followed it round to the gate. The caretaker's door was shut, and there was no one about in the yard with its litter of metal shavings, but outside the offices the boss's white car was parked. Behind the sheds the hydraulic press was thumping away.

'Swallowing the last bits of the grey lorry,' Cady joked. 'But there's bound to be something left over.'

He stopped outside the gate, made up his mind and tugged the rusty bell-pull. This set off a furious jangling outside the caretaker's door. Out popped Big Jules, who showed the same surprise as had his opposite-number at Demagny's Warehouses.

'Am I dreaming? So now you've come to cheek us on our own doorstep, have you? Just you get out of it and look sharp, too, or I'll get my cosh!'

'We're waiting,' Cady retorted and pulled the bell again.

Its jangling echoed round the yard. Anxious faces peered out of the sheds. Jules came leaping over to the gate.

'Let go of that chain or I'll lay you out cold.'

'Take it easy!' Sandra told him. 'We haven't come to cheek you.'

She had no thought now of running away.

'We just wanted to see the Scrap-metal King,' Cady added soothingly.

Big Jules let the cosh slip to his side and stared at them in amazement.

'No! I can't have heard properly. You really want to see Monsieur Kovacovici?'

'Himself, in person, and not the office-boy, either.'

'What do you want with him?'

'That's his business,' Cady replied. 'If you're scared to go and get him, just let us in. We shan't pinch anything out of your sheds: food's the only thing we're interested in.'

Big Jules' purple face widened into a suspicious grin.

'That's a good idea! I'll take you over to the office myself. As it happens the boss has a small account to settle with the pair of you. In you go!'

He opened the gate and escorted them across the yard, swinging his cosh threateningly.

'Up the steps like good little children, and don't try to run away: it's too late now!'

He pushed open the first door he came to.

'Guess who I've brought to see you? The two crazy kids from the shanty-town.'

The Mangler was sprawled in a leather armchair, his feet on the desk. His green hat was on the back of his head and he was wearing an oil-stained sheepskin jacket. He twitched his newspaper aside. At first he was too astonished to utter a word. Then a smile spread across his grease-spotted red face.

'How nice of them to walk right into the lion's den! Now we've only got to make up our minds how we'd like to serve them up. If you ask me the first thing we ought to do is tenderize their horrid little hides with a belt-strap. Old Fred and the Crocodile would be only too happy to put their men on that job.'

Suddenly he swung his legs off the desk, slowly heaved himself out of his armchair, and brought his ugly face close to Sandra and Cady.

'What do you think of that?'

Sandra did not give much for their chances and Cady was beginning to lose faith in his luck. It looked as though the arguments which he had successfully used against Monsieur Alexandre would not work with a man of somewhat limited brain-power.

'Before you do anything else,' he said weakly, 'I think you should listen to us.'

'I'm listening. What's it all about?'

'We're just going round collecting funds for our school, and we thought you might give as much as your neighbours have done.'

The Mangler blocked his ears, then raised his fists to the ceiling, and finally called for his fifteen villains (or rather fourteen since the enforced retirement of Philippon), holders over the past six years of an enviable record of 271 lorries stolen in the Paris area alone, including the unlucky grey one brought in by the Dormouse.

'You heard that! These two agitators corrupt the shanty-town so that we lose two thousand francs alone in rent for November! But as if that isn't enough, they've got the nerve to come round here and beg for that wooden shack they use as a pigsty for the snotty-nosed little brats of Bois-Bréau. No! No! No!'

But Cady had a one-track mind and he thought the time had come to strike the decisive blow.

'Monsieur Alexandre gave me two hundred francs.'

He pulled aside his oilskins to give them a distant view of the booty, at the same time keeping a careful eye on Big Jules. The Scrap-metal King's face twitched.

'He must have gone crazy!'

'Oh no, he didn't. The boss of Demagny's Warehouses took a bit of talking round at first, but then he was very pleased to make his contribution in return for something useful.'

'What do you mean?'

'I gave him a couple of bits of information worth a good sight more than two hundred francs: we didn't want to exploit the position. If you're interested in that sort of a deal, we could arrange something on the same terms.'

There was a frankness about the way in which Cady spoke which disguised his cunning. The Mangler was completely taken in by this.

'You've something interesting to tell me?'

'Of course I have. But you must keep your side of the deal.'

'It's a promise,' said the scrap-merchant.

He had already made up his mind that he would pay the two spies with a clout on the head and then boot them out of the office.

'Well, shall we shake on it, then?' Cady asked and held out his right hand. 'I know that means more than any signature.'

The Scrap-metal King gave Cady's hand a slap and regretted it bitterly. Cady now plunged bravely in.

'Monsieur Alexandre now knows all about the unfortunate blunder your men made the other night while your back was turned. I mean the brand-new Willème Filochard and the Dormouse brought back to your yard instead of abandoning ten miles away down some dark street. And don't forget the grey lorry had a passenger aboard who flew away.'

The Mangler's jaw dropped slightly and his bloodshot eyes became dark slits of anxiety.

'That can't be,' he said uncertainly. 'I saw my old pal Alexandre and we just talked of this and that. If he'd known, he'd have marked me for life. Who told him?'

Cady sadly shook his head.

'I'm the one who spilled the beans.'

He put up his arms to ward off the first blow, but the Mangler was too astonished to move and simply slumped back into his chair. The silence within the room could be felt. Big Jules took one step back and then another, as he melted away from the scene. The Mangler leaned forward, stared at Sandra and Cady and clenched his huge fists. Under his green hat his face was pale and bloodless.

'I'll strangle you with my bare hands,' he gasped. 'Then I'll give you to Big Fred and his men to put into the hydraulic press. Bois-Bréau will be freed for good and all of you and your schemings.'

Then Cady put the finishing touch to the stroke which countered this attractive programme.

'You'd be making a big mistake. I'll tell you why. Because sooner or later Monsieur Alexandre would have got hold of the story from one of your men. Now, thanks to me, you can get ahead of him in settling scores, if necessary prepare your defence and perhaps skip the country before he does, when the time comes to make your getaway.'

The Mangler did not appear to accept such a disaster.

'The balloon's going up very soon now,' Cady insisted.

'That's just another of your fairy-stories!'

'No, it isn't. This time it's something Sandra found out. She's mighty sensitive to danger, no matter where it's brewing, from your scrap-yard or from outside.'

The Mangler turned to Sandra, who hit the target at once.

'The fuzz are in Bois-Bréau!'

'You're bluffing! I'd have known the moment they stuck their noses in . . .'

'Fat Théo would have told you? He's useless; solid bone from the neck up. This very morning Monsieur Chabot came round and got him to let the Poles' shack to a couple of strangers, the Lambert brothers. Said they were truck drivers. My foot! A kid of ten could have guessed where they came from. Plain-clothes men from the ghost-squad. You can bet the rest of them are hanging round Saint-Ouen waiting for the tip-off.'

'Did you see them?' the Mangler asked the boy.

'Only in the distance, and I didn't like the look of them.'

Cady was still not sure that he had really unnerved the scrap-merchant, for the ugliness of his face was a mask which made it hard to determine his true reactions. All the same, this change of attitude showed that he was slipping slightly. With someone like this, frankness could be a useful card to play. He went on with the same devil-may-care boldness.

'Not a soul in the village likes you, you know, and I expect it's the same in the scrap-yard. But that doesn't mean that people don't admit one good point about you, that it's thanks to you and the way you get round the regulations that Bois-Bréau has been able to carry on for so long as it has, without the local authorities threatening to close it down. Everyone realises that once you go, their security goes too. Less than a fortnight ago I saw Moulin-Noir cleared in a morning, all because the police had arrested the boss of the shanty-town, a man just like you. Places like that can't run for ever unless they've got someone tough to run them. That's why we came to warn you—in return for a small contribution.'

He watched the scrap-merchant out of the corner of his eye to see what effect his yarn had had, and then added calmly:

'It's well worth a couple of hundred francs.'

'A hundred and fifty, and not a penny more!' The Mangler gave a dying gasp.

He seemed to be thinking about something else as he stared at the opposite wall with dull, astonished eyes. The suspense lasted for several seconds, while Cady and Sandra anxiously waited. Then his hand went to his jacket, produced a grimy wad of banknotes, opened it exactly at dead centre, took out the two which he had earlier extorted from Madame Meunier, handed them to a quick-snatching Cady, put his cash away and zipped his sheepskin jacket up again. All this was done so abstractedly as to make one wonder whether he had caught a disease which he had never known before, the slow growth of fear.

'Go away!'

He spoke in a different voice, but Cady was sharp enough to realise that the change might not last long and he signed to Sandra. They were glad to slip out of the room, down the steps and across the width of the yard. It was like walking the tight-rope and their courage only came back when they were a yard or two from the gate. They stopped to get their breath and looked back. The hydraulic press no longer broke the silence and the men who worked it stood motionless at the controls, their eyes on the gateway. Meanwhile Old Fred and his men and the two drivers lurked in the doorway of the furthest shed, but their stillness now betrayed their astonishment as much as their uncertainty.

The Mangler emerged from his lair and stood at the top of the steps as if mesmerised, unable to believe that his visitors had gone. The only word they heard came from Big Jules' lips as he stood in his porch:

'You little devils! If you come hanging round here again, I'll make mincemeat of you! Get out!'

They raced across the road and dived into the undergrowth. A delayed-action reflex of fear gripped Sandra and she looked in horror at Cady.

'It's a miracle we got out of that horrible place, and all you can do is laugh!'

'Why not? We didn't pinch anything or smash anything. We just chatted to the Mangler for a minute or two and we didn't use a single swear-word. And yet we can use just as many as Fatty or the Crocodile when we're really worked up.'

The gipsies appeared, knocking the snow from the low branches.

'You all right?' Zalko asked in an anxious voice. 'We've been scared about you.'

'Not a scratch,' Sandra answered. 'In normal times, we'd have only come out feet first.'

'Any money?'

'We've got that. The Mangler gave almost as much as that crook at Demagny's. I just don't know how Cady managed it, but they let him have his way as easy as kiss my hand. Look at that!'

Cady was delighted to show them the banknotes; there was no false modesty about him.

'We had to take a risk, but we were lucky we were dealing with people who were so certain that nothing could ever upset them, they went about with their eyes shut. A word or two from me, and they were scared out of their wits.'

'Let's go straight back to the school,' Sandra suggested. 'The Guardian Angel must be worrying himself stiff about us.'

II

The Night Visitors

SLOWLY AND imperceptibly the snow began to drift down once more from the dark sky and its magic enchanted the children as they came out of school. Monsieur Langelin stood in the doorway and watched them for some minutes as they went leaping like demons down the street. He was about to go indoors again when suddenly the older children were all around him, their eyes lit with joy. Somebody thrust some banknotes into his hand. He turned them over and over as he listened impassively to the account the collectors gave him: when they'd finished, he gave his verdict.

'Take it back. It's stolen money.'

'But we didn't steal it!' Cady protested. 'It's no business of ours where it comes from. Anyway, Sandra can tell you, I didn't get it by threats. They gave it perfectly freely! We should be proper mugs if we turned up our noses at a nice bit of cash, half of which probably came from Bois-Bréau in the first place. Madame Meunier would agree with me.'

With some embarrassment the Guardian Angel took back the money. Cady tried to appease him.

'Your Jesus would never have tortured his conscience like you've been doing. He wouldn't have minded sharing out money from thieves among the poor people round him.'

'You aren't Jesus,' the Guardian Angel retorted drily.

'When he was my age,' Cady replied, 'I bet he didn't

think very much of older people either. You're a priest, so why don't you bless those banknotes and make them all right. Tomorrow the nurse can turn them into bread and milk.'

Around him Sandra and the gipsies, the Boubarka brothers and their friends, Violet and Rosie, Beppo Torrente and Serafina, Mimile Rouvier and Pimpin Léonard, César Mahmadou and his two younger brothers, all waited to see what he would do. The Guardian Angel's lips moved, he made the sign of the cross over the notes and then put them into his wallet.

'That reminds me,' he added. 'We've still got a couple of tins of liver paste in the surgery cupboard. The others left half a loaf, so we could make ourselves some sandwiches while Cady heats the soup.'

The dog's hairy muzzle popped out immediately from under the camp-bed. His reactions to news of a meal had become automatic. Above, the myna on the beam flapped its wings and called insults down on the visitors.

'Come in all of you, and shut the door behind you,' Monsieur Langelin called cheerfully. 'Let's enjoy ourselves for a minute or two.'

The Lambert brothers had spent the afternoon wandering around the shanty-town, going from alley to alley to meet the locals, chatting for a moment with the out-of-work Portuguese, saying hullo to the Algerians at the frontier of the Wadi Radam, gossiping with the housewives waiting for the potatoes to come in at Bofano's grocery and, of course, occasionally passing through the door of the canteen where Fat Théo served them mulled wine and complaints about life in general.

There was nothing suspicious about the way in which they killed time, although it was noticeable that they would stop for some time outside the less gloomy or less dilapidated shacks. They would light cigarettes, staring around and listening to the household noises which came through the half-open windows.

After one last call at the 'Eldorado' at about five they walked up to the very end of the Champs-Elysées to look at the gipsies' encampment and the most wretched corner of the shanty-town, the village of rotten canvas which served as a temporary shelter for the workless Africans. César Mahmadou had gone back to his tent after the gang had scattered, and he saw them walk back down the sunken road and stop inquisitively outside the Green House. A faint yellow light still glowed through the tiny, frost-encrusted windows.

Monsieur Langelin was alone there with Cady and Sandra, all three chattering away cheerfully. Their laughter ceased abruptly when they heard whispering and the shuffle of feet outside.

'Our old friends the scrap-men making their last round,' the Guardian Angel muttered anxiously.

'They've got other things to think about now,' Cady hastened to reassure him. 'They've forgotten about Bois-Bréau. They won't even spare the time to set fire to the village before they cut and run.'

Sandra half-opened the door and recognised the figures standing outside in the darkness and the snow. She had as little love for the police as she had for the crooks who for the past six years had exploited the wretched working-people of the shanty-town.

'What are you looking for?'

'We were just wondering what was inside this building,' the elder of the two admitted.

'It's the school,' Sandra answered crossly. 'In cold weather it's used as a day-nursery as well. Sick and injured people come here for treatment, too. Do you want to look at it?'

Monsieur Langelin had come to the door.

'Come in,' he said. 'There's nothing to see, except the paintings the children have done and the games which help me to keep them amused.'

Pignouf lay on the camp-bed. He growled to himself when he saw the strangers and then relapsed into his blissful state of indolence.

'Not so bad,' said the younger of the pair. 'I reckon you wouldn't expect to find a school in a place like this.'

'It cost me more trouble than money,' the Guardian Angel admitted, refusing to taking offence.

Once Sandra had shut the door, she leaned her back against it and stared perplexedly at the couple. There was something about the Lambert brothers which suggested they were ordinary people and not plain-clothes men, for they had none of the steely detachment which usually shows through the good manners and the disguise of a policeman. Both were warmly clad like truck-drivers, but their thick, wool-lined jerkins showed no stain or tear, and their aura of cleanliness was surprising in people supposed to drive their heavy vehicles through all the mud of a building site.

The elder grinned at Cady, who was just finishing his sandwich, and patted the dog. The younger followed Monsieur Langelin down the centre aisle and listened politely to what he told him. When he reached the master's desk he noticed a slight fault in the walls which formed a sort of apse at the end of the room.

'The place is built of bits and pieces,' he said with a smile, 'and it looks as though your architect had to change his mind quite a lot.'

'The original idea,' the Guardian Angel admitted, 'was for the building to be used both as school and chapel. The people who live and work here know only the wages of their work and the landlord's impositions. They let me take care of their children, but only in a school, not a chapel.'

'Oh,' said the younger man, somewhat embarrassed.

Mechanically he stared up at the beams and the scanty roofing of corrugated iron through which the cold came down in waves. Sandra noticed where he was looking and she spotted the myna perched in his usual place, one bright eye fixed upon the intruder.

'That isn't the Holy Ghost,' she said with a laugh, 'although he has the gift of tongues.'

Anxiously, Cady turned towards them. He was ready to step in, but he had no time, for suddenly the bird came swooping down, and without a moment's hesitation settled on the stranger's shoulder, its beak close to his ear.

'Hi, Charlie! forgotten your little friend?'

'Hullo, Igor!' the man answered with a guffaw. 'So you still remember your old dad!'

They chatted happily together and the myna soon raised his voice to call for drinks all round. Cady came up to the group by the master's desk.

'Put him down!' he choked. 'The bird chose me. I'm the only one he obeys.'

'No, Igor belongs to me.'

'But who are you?'

'His owner, Charlie Rouvet, and this is my mate.'

'Hullo, me old Gaston!' Igor squawked.

'Hullo, you old devil,' the older man replied.

'Step on it mates, another hour on the road and we'll be at Mother Dutilleul's—yippee!'

'Shut up,' said Cady. 'I suppose you'd like to end the day with a skewer through your guts. Listen to him; he's going to wake everyone up! Then we'll have the scrapmen down on us like a ton of bricks.'

'Quiet!' croaked Igor. 'Or I'll have the lot of you inside!'

You could no longer hear yourself speak as this reunion ceremony dissolved into a howl of laughter. When everyone, including the talkative bird, had recovered, Sandra took the floor.

'I thought you were the fuzz,' she announced, facing the two men with some embarrassment.

'We're not far off it, you know,' Charlie replied. 'For the last two days we've been beating up and down between Argenteuil and Sartrouville on the lookout for our lorry.'

'It's just round the corner,' Cady told them. 'But it's in bits and pieces.'

'We'll get our money back on the Willème,' said Gaston Perrot. 'As far as both we and the police are concerned the main thing is to find where it's been hidden, and then who stole it. We guessed that easily enough by making that fat fool who runs the canteen talk.'

'You hit the jackpot there,' Monsieur Langelin cheerfully admitted. 'But you had to get to Bois-Bréau first. Who tipped you off?'

Charlie pointed to the myna perched on his shoulder.

'Igor, through a third party.'

'That's impossible!' Sandra exclaimed. 'Once he'd left the cab of your lorry, Igor followed us down to the village and has been with us ever since.'

But Cady was thinking, a far-away look in his eyes.

'That's it!' he said suddenly. 'Don't you remember what we did that night? We came back along the main road, watching them towing the Willème in the distance. We went over the cross-roads to meet the Portuguese in the sunken road. Igor wasn't with us then. We saw him again fifteen minutes later, outside the Green House, and we don't know what he was up to in the meantime.'

Sandra sniggered.

'I expect he popped into the nearest bar to ring you up!'

165

'No, he didn't,' Charlie said. 'But what he did do amounts to much the same thing.'

'You're not having us on?'

'No, I'm not. Around this time several lorries coming from Pontoise were held up by an obstruction at the Croix-Souci cross-roads.'

'We spotted that!' Cady interrupted. 'The scrap-men's breakdown truck was crawling along towing the Willème, and they were the ones who stopped the traffic. What happened next?'

'Igor went fluttering over and suddenly perched in the window of a heavy lorry. You can imagine how startled the crew were when he began saying his party-piece. Then the traffic began to move again and he disappeared once more. Some days later, when the driver had seen the newspaper-story about the theft of the lorry and its mascot, he phoned the paper to say where they'd met him. "We saw Igor on 2 December, at six in the evening on Highway 192, close to the junction with the main road from Epinay." You can imagine how the cops leaped at that; it gave them a first-rate start to their investigations. They've kept under cover so far, for fear of frightening their suspects, but you can bet that when they do strike, they'll come down hard on the Scrap-metal King and all he owns.'

Cady was not in the least concerned about the lorry-thieves who had flourished for the past six years in the suburbs of Paris, though their fate had been settled the day he turned up in Bois-Bréau. The clue to their discovery had been the pair of wellingtons given to him by the only crook with a spark of decency, in a moment of pity such as must have occurred seldom among the villains in the scrap-yard.

'What are you going to do with Igor?'

'I'll take him away with me now,' Charlie answered.

He opened the zipper of his jerkin and at once the myna came down to snuggle against his chest.

'We'll miss him,' Sandra said with a catch in her voice. 'He gave us a lot of fun.'

And then she told the story of the Mangler and his men, and how they chased in and out of the alleys of the shanty-town in pursuit of a dead crow which two jokers had been pulling on a string. Old Gaston and Charlie laughed and laughed.

'You haven't lost everything,' Charlie said, producing his wallet. 'I still owe you what I promised to pay.'

They had quite forgotten the reward. Sandra's eyes opened wide as she took the five hundred francs and, quite forgetting Cady, brought the money over to the Guardian Angel.

The two lorry-drivers departed with warm expressions of their goodwill.

'We shan't even spend one night in the village,' Gaston Perrot announced. 'The first thing to do is to make Fat Théo cough up, collect our traps and then get a bed in Mareuil. The cops are waiting for us there. It's safe to tell you that the raid is timed for tomorrow morning.'

Once the door had shut, the Guardian Angel handed the money to Cady.

'You got us the cash, so it's up to you to spend it as you like.'

'It belongs to us all. Charlie was just paying Igor's board and lodging. That long-nosed clown was your guest, not mine.'

'What's upset you?'

'I make friends too easily,' Cady admitted. 'And when it's time to say goodbye, I don't like it.'

'A good night's sleep will help you forget it. And think how pleased Madame Meunier will be tomorrow morning when she finds this small fortune you two have collected in such a short time.'

'Sandra and I hoped for nothing less.'

They escorted their Guardian Angel outside and watched him fly off on his scooter. The snow was coming down in a thick blanket, blotting out the scattered lights of the shanty-town.

'Come and sleep in our place,' Sandra offered. 'Granny and grand-dad have been in a better temper these last few days.'

'I'd be too scared of being a nuisance,' Cady replied. 'And anyway I wouldn't want to leave the dog all by himself in the Green House. The Guardian Angel would be cross about it.'

Sandra gave him a kiss on the cheek and then vanished like a shadow into the snowstorm. Pignouf came up to his master in the doorway, sniffed the cold air and wagged his tail. He then looked up at the boy, as much as to ask, 'Anything good on the menu tonight?'

'The usual,' Cady muttered. 'Rhinoceros stew and spuds. The only place I've ever eaten meat like that is in this shanty-town of yours. I expect it's horse: but a horse that died in a ditch of old age!'

Much later the three witches from the gipsy encampment came in, despite the snow. Cady was sleeping beside the dog in bed. He scarcely heard the swishing sound of their long skirts against the benches, but after a moment or two he opened one eye. The little lamp on the corner of the desk was lit and its red flame set fantastic shadows dancing between the beams and the roof. Blissfully he went to sleep again, carrying this picture from one dream to the next.

168

12

A Good Hole
to Hide in

'THEY'VE GONE!'

From door to door the news ran down the Champs-
Elysées. It had originated with the gipsies, for their
encampment was best situated to hear the traffic start up
at dawn. There had been ten police-cars all told. They
moved almost silently as they crossed the Croix-Souci
junction and took up a strategic position midway between
the fence round the scrap-yard and the great iron gates of
Demagny's Warehouses, but their sirens wailed in
triumph as they sped back to Paris with a cargo of
prisoners aboard. Caught fast asleep, the scrap-men had
put up as little resistance as the highly respected gentlemen next door, or Fat Théo and his two strong-arm men
hauled from the 'Eldorado' by a massive pair in dark
overcoats.

'THEY'VE GONE!'

It was barely light. Sandra was awakened by the cry
and instantly felt done out of one bitter pleasure—the
sight of the whole gang walking up the main road in
clanking chains towards a black maria. A little later she
had the consolation of an unexpected sight on the opposite
side of the road—the warehouse gates gaping like a
breach blown in the wall of a fortress, and those of the
scrap-yard swinging on their hinges.

The people who lived in the shanty-town still could not

169

believe that they were free, for this was something they had never known before. Grandfather Rouvier himself had little confidence that life would be any easier.

'I know that skunk Horace Kovacovici. Nobody can beat him when it comes to getting a case dismissed. Some idiotic magistrate will let him off and he'll be back with his gorillas in a couple of days. Then it's back to the treadmill for us! They ought to kill them! Every single one of them! But we aren't murderers!'

Mimile ran to the corner of the main street to take the temperature of public opinion, excitedly kissed any of his friends or their mothers whom he met, even the ugliest of them, and returned to shout once more at the top of his voice:

'THEY'VE GONE!'

The old couple would not be convinced.

'Out!' his grandmother shouted from beside the stove. 'Take your bread and butter and go and get me a quart of milk from Bofano's.'

At the foot of the Champs-Elysées beside the Wadi Radam the first flag flew. It was only a rag of red nylon, but in an instant every window in the street had its standard flying, flags of all colours neatly cut from cast-off underwear. The men went off to work through streets dressed overall, with the prospect of coming home that night for the first time without trouble or disturbance. The 'Eldorado' was open to the winds. On their way to work they tapped Fat Théo's barrels and emptied on the spot such bottles on the bar as had survived the earlier disaster.

'That's not right!' old Monsieur Rouvier exclaimed as he cheerfully kicked his workmates out of the canteen. 'You'll have the police asking us to settle for the damage we've done.'

Behind his words was the rooted honesty of generations

170

of countrymen, who could see no difference between the evil done by a bad man and the revenge taken by his victims.

'Horace is dead!' one of them shouted at him.

'And the way you're carrying on will bring him back to life again!' the old man retorted.

Although she did not show it, Sandra entirely approved of his attitude. Behind her, a swarm of shanty-town children talked of burning the 'Eldorado' to the ground.

'No,' she told them, 'now they've gone, nobody's going to be punished any more. Four or five families could live in comfort in this fine big hut built from our rents. Go off to the Africans right now and fetch César Mahmadou. He can tell us who are the worst off, starting with himself, of course.'

'THEY'VE GONE!'

Despite the snow which half hid the flags in the Champs-Elysées and muffled the sounds of rejoicing coming from even the gloomiest alleys, Monsieur Langelin guessed what had happened the moment he saw two pine-branches nailed in the form of a cross on the door of the Green House. There was nobody at home. The nurse had not yet arrived, while Cady had taken the dog out to join in the celebrations of liberation-day, no doubt.

The cross could not have been there long, for the snowflakes barely covered the thick mass of pine needles. As he entered his lair the Guardian Angel wondered who could have done it. He shivered. The stove had gone out. The thin blanket which lay neatly folded on the camp-bed was stiff and cold.

Monsieur Langelin sighed deeply. Boy, dog and bird had all been together one morning, and all gone the next! It was not fair, when he had done so much to give life and soul to a place lacking the smallest comfort.

171

Suddenly behind him there came the faintest clink of a bracelet. He looked round, and to his surprise, there in the doorway stood the three witches from the gipsy camp, long skirts and striped shawls cloaking them like statues against the snowy morning. It was the first time they had ventured near the Green House in daylight. Events had driven them from the warmth of their caravans and sharpened their curiosity. The Guardian Angel understood the position at once, and thanked them for the cross of pine-branches.

'Where is He?' one of them asked, making the sign of the cross.

At first the Guardian Angel thought that she meant Cady, whom they had passed so often, with his faithful if unfortunate hound and the crazy bird who made them all laugh. Then everything became mixed up inside his poor head.

'He is everywhere!' he said, flinging wide his arms to embrace the shanty-town as well as the Green House now open to the half-light which poured through the door and gave its interior the appearance of the nave of a church.

The gipsy-women knelt in silence to receive his clumsily-phrased blessing.

'I've even forgotten how to say mass,' he humbly admitted. 'The wretchedness of the place has left me with no time for this kind of prayer. Come in! We'll have a cup of coffee together and break bread at breakfast. It will come to just the same thing. This is the mass I have been saying every morning for the last four or five years with the toddlers of Bois-Bréau. Will they ever believe in something less ugly than the life around them? We cannot tell. But I am sure that they will never forget the daily gift of food, their lessons, the songs and laughter of their earliest days.'

It was a simple ceremony and it was right and proper

that the old ladies should keep their distance when they were given a cup of coffee which was not so sweet as they might have expected, and the slice of dry bread which the Guardian Angel cut for them.

'Cady and the dog have had my last tin of meat,' he said, to put them at their ease.

They smiled discreetly and gazed at him with eyes which shone with reverent interest.

'May we come back?' asked old Granny Zalko.

'As you always do,' he answered with a grin, 'with your duplicate key. But from this evening you will have to leave your lamp behind.'

They talked then of the Mangler and his followers.

'Can you forgive them for what they've done to us here?' asked Monsieur Langelin.

The question remained for some minutes in suspense. Then Granny Gomez answered for her companions and for everyone in the village.

'No! But it's different for you. I expect you have to believe that those wretches have repented.'

'I'll never hear confessions from a worse bunch of villains than those,' the Guardian Angel said with a smile. 'And I must admit that I'd find it rather hard to give them absolution. My own indulgence has its up and downs. In the morning, I'm ready to forgive everybody when I open the place to the children who may lack everything but still do not know what hatred is. In the evening, when I have to go out alone into the darkness and the cold, knowing how ineffective I am, then I can forgive nothing.'

Suddenly the old ladies scuttled away as they heard the 2 CV coming down the track. Madame Meunier was repaid for all her thousand and one disappointments when she saw the bunting in the windows along the main street, the cross of branches nailed to the door of the Green House and the smile on the face of the Guardian Angel.

'Have they gone?' she asked feebly.

'At dawn, and well guarded. We are free of them! They'll never come back. Now the children can come to us without that hangdog look. Of course poverty won't be banished from Bois-Bréau overnight, but people will be able to lead a more decent life, and prepare for better days to come.'

But Madame Meunier had not got over her surprise.

'Why did they go so quickly?'

'The police are always in a hurry.' Monsieur Langelin laughed gently at her. 'I hope the net was drawn tightly round the lot of them and that none of the big fish managed to swim away.'

As was usual each morning at about this time the first of the children came walking hand in hand down the street. They were chirping like real sparrows and you could see the grins on their faces from far away.

Suddenly Madame Meunier felt sorry.

'We've nothing to give them to celebrate the occasion. They won't give me credit at Mareuil. Do you think old Bofano would help us out? I should like to have something special for the little ones.'

The Guardian Angel produced his wallet.

'Somebody has already taken care of that. Don't you want to know who?'

He did not interrupt the silence which ensued, until he looked down, smiled and said:

'I wouldn't deceive you. Let's say that Cady undertook a fund-raising campaign for us. Take the money, get back into that old rattle-trap of yours and fetch a stack of good things.'

The older children worked all day helping some of the women move into a group of brand-new huts which Fat Théo had adamantly refused to let. After that they drew lots for the Poles' shack and luck favoured the Torrentes, fair compensation for what they had been through a few days before.

Weary but happy, the children made their way back to the Green House a little before five and were welcomed with open arms by the Guardian Angel. He no longer had the heart to scold anyone, as lemonade and hot chocolate were drunk and Madame Meunier handed out sandwiches with such delicious flavours as had never been tasted before in Bois-Bréau. Emboldened by the holiday atmosphere, the little ones came up one after the other to the master's desk to do their turn—a poem learned by heart and recited with great effort, a simple song accompanied by the chaplain's guitar, or an imitation of one of the villains hauled out of bed at crack of dawn by the men of the ghost squad. The audience had to guess.

It was only too easy, and jeers and boos from the audience greeted a little six- or eight-year-old's impersonation of Fat Théo, the Crocodile, Battling Flagada, Felletin the Cosh and the Mangler. But first prize for imitations went without any argument to Pimpin Léonard whose throat produced all the backchat the myna had given them from the beams of the Green House—and elsewhere.

Igor might have flown away for ever, but they cheered him just as loudly. It was after this that the Guardian Angel and Madame Meunier noticed some of the children sitting in the back row looking dejected.

'Where's Cady?' they asked Sandra and Simbad, as the others went home.

'He's gone,' Sandra answered with a catch in her voice. 'And he's taken the dog with him.'

She began to cry silently. The Algerian stood beside her. The Guardian Angel took them gently by the arm and closed the door.

'When?'

'We don't know. He was still around the place at mid-day, but nobody saw him push off. Cady went as he came—without a scrap of food in his belly.'

'It can't be true,' Madame Meunier objected. 'Why should he have left us?'

'I think,' Saïd Boubarka expressed his considered opinion, 'I think that there was nothing more left for him to do in Bois-Bréau. That's why he shoved off.'

'We must get him back!' the Guardian Angel exclaimed.

This made Sandra smile once more through her tears.

'You can always try, but he moves fast.'

Pignouf had not lost his sense of smell like some old gun-dogs whom their masters spoil at the fireside. Past abandoned factories, over wasteland, he made a bee-line for the sidings at Argenteuil, where Cady had noticed some ancient carriages when he had first entered this heaven-blessed land a fortnight before.

It was growing dark and it was snowing again, thick, slow flurries which would suddenly blot out the lights in the suburbs around. It was cold, and boy and dog began to feel very hungry indeed. Cady had enough bread in his pockets to last them a couple of days and had also lifted a tin of meat from one of the Guardian Angel's boxes.

'In a minute,' he said and patted Pignouf's hairy head.

Wisely they stopped some distance from the railway embankment. There was not a light nor the slightest sign of life showing. The carriages stood out black against the snow. Cady set his fingers to his lips and gave a shrill whistle. They watched the shattered carriage windows and waited, but nothing moved and still not a light showed. The very tramps had deserted this mournful shelter for the underground stations on the outskirts of

176

Paris with their long warm passages where the rush-hour crowds could be conned out of some small change.

'Let's pick a good one,' Cady muttered.

They walked along the train which had stopped for ever and finally discovered a venerable old sleeping-coach which must have dated back to 1910. Long ago this relic of the Orient Express had been cleared of its padded cushions, its mirrors and its varnished partitions. One compartment alone remained closed, and it was littered with the heaps of straw and rags left by other wanderers. The dog growled and would not go in.

Cady struck a match and held the fluttering flame high above his head.

'Get out!' a voice growled from the gloom. 'Let me sleep in peace . . . '

The man lying there in the filth was either drunk or utterly exhausted, but he sat up abruptly as the match went out. Cady had blown it out swiftly and had slipped into the corridor, feeling his way through the darkness.

His heart pounded as he wondered if he had been recognised. But a resolve, stronger than his fear, prevented him from running away. Still growling, the dog was at his heels and this noise could give away their position. Cady bent down in the darkness to pat him, to stroke the hair stiff with rage and gently to muzzle him with his hand. Pignouf quietened at once.

And so they reached the carriage door gaping onto the snow-covered embankment. There was not a sound behind them. Cady leaned out to watch the other end for the figure which could suddenly jump down on to the ballast and vanish among the tracks. He was determined to follow, no matter how long the chase or how far it took him. The tension grew unbearably for a few seconds, and then at last from the end of the corridor came the sound of a man's voice.

177

'I know where you're hiding! You move, and I'll put a bullet through your brains. Who are you?'

Cady took good care not to answer. More and more scared though he had become, he had not lost his instinct of self-preservation. He heard the man cock his pistol, but the click of the bolt reassured him, for it showed that the other was on the verge of panic.

'I'll shoot! There's nine rounds in the magazine. I may miss with the first, but the rest will get you.'

The Mangler crouched in his corner. He had escaped the dawn raid by the skin of his teeth and he was anxious at all costs to remain free so that he could start to organise his legal defence. The police were everywhere. They had set up road-blocks. In the end he had found refuge in this graveyard of rolling-stock, high above another set of factories and another stretch of wasteland.

For twelve hours he had been on the run, twisting and turning in the snow and the bitter north wind. Two million francs' worth of banknotes were taped to his chest but were of no use to him now. Cold and exhaustion had brought him low and, to make matters worse, he was horribly, horribly hungry.

Cady could feel the dog tense under his hand. A heavy tread came closer, ever so slowly closer, trampling the rubbish strewn along the corridor. There was only one way out, through the door leading along the train, and then a mad dash among the deserted carriages, which provided a thousand hiding-places. But which of the two was the hunter? 'I am,' Cady thought, keeping absolutely still, 'and I'll drive him into a place that he'll never get out of.'

Slowly the Mangler reached the end of the carriage without having noticed the slightest movement around him. He wondered if the prowler had cleared off by now. The dim light reflected from the snow came through the open door and showed the glass-panelled swing-door at the end, leading to the next coach. Somebody was behind it, watching his every move. It was only the dimmest outline, but instantly the Mangler recognised the face which smiled at him. His pistol came up and he fired.

The glass shattered, and with it Cady's reflection. The Mangler had no time to mourn this killing. A coarse-haired wolf leaped for his throat and brought him to the floor. The jaws with their long teeth gripped tight. He struggled to reach the pistol which had fallen to one side, but as his fingers closed on the butt, down came Cady's boot. He shrieked in agony and lost consciousness.

His awakening was less painful. The floor of the coach had been carefully swept and in the middle of it sparkled a little fire made of chips of wood. The flickering light revealed the dog's hairy muzzle and the rather more agreeable features of its master. Cady was sitting on the floor cross-legged, spreading meat-paste on slices of bread. He gave some to the dog, put his knife on the tin and then began to eat himself. Both chewed away contentedly and gazed happily at one another.

The Mangler coughed and heaved himself up on one elbow.

'It's no good looking for your gun.' The boy spoke with his mouth full. 'It's somewhere under the snow, fifty yards away from the carriage. If you move the dog will get you, he knows the way to your double chin, and I'll bring this iron bar on top of your head. This is our place and we don't want any trouble here.'

'I'm awfully hungry!' the Mangler groaned.

'It's never too late to swallow your troubles. It'll do you a world of good.'

Nevertheless he put some paste on to a scrap of bread and carefully handed it over.

179

'Poor man's caviare! Don't turn up your nose at it.'

The Mangler made one mouthful of it, and as he chewed it his spirits revived.

'You've got to get me out of this! I've got money, plenty of it, and anything you do for me I'll pay you well.'

Cady pointed to the end of the coach.

'There are only two ways out of here. Turn right and you'll be back in Bois-Bréau where they're waiting for you: turn left and you'll be on the road to Argenteuil.'

'Splendid!' the Mangler exclaimed. 'That's the safest way to go. You call a taxi and I'll give you five hundred francs.'

'You wouldn't get a hundred yards. The fuzz are everywhere. But I can take you to a safe place, where your tracks would disappear as fast as snow in the Sahara. Is that what you want?'

Cady spoke so confidently that the Mangler dragged himself to his feet. He followed the boy and the dog along the snow-covered embankment overlooking a tract of darkness in which twinkled scattered lights. As he walked along the Mangler could see through the snowflakes a landscape oddly like the hollow of Bois-Bréau.

'The shanty-town of La Frette,' Cady explained. 'Reserved for tramps, unemployed and men on the run. Very hospitable they are, and they keep their mouths shut. Never given anyone away. You stay with them and you'll have plenty of time to see how things pan out.'

He set two fingers to his lips and whistled. At once Horace Kovacovici saw the gleam of a host of eyes like fireflies below him. Laughter and mocking shouts rose from below.

'No!' the Mangler bellowed, recoiling in alarm.

'Yes! In your position it's just the place you need.'

Cady pushed with all his strength. The Mangler teetered on the edge of the embankment, lost his balance,

180

rolled clumsily down the slope and tumbled into the midst of the human wolves who lived in La Frette. With an angry roar the pack closed on their prey.

'Take good care of him!' Cady shouted to them. 'He's got enough to pay for his board and lodging till Christmas 2000!'

It was the first Sunday of a new era in Bois-Bréau. The chimney-smoke drifted up into the still air and the carpet of snow hid the ugly surroundings. The Guardian Angel stood at the top of the track and surveyed for some time the domain where hopeless day had succeeded so many other hopeless days.

Then he wheeled his scooter down the slope, respecting the peaceful silence in which the village was still wrapped. No sacrilegious hand had dared to violate the cross of pine-branches which the old heathens had nailed to the door of the Green House. This was a good sign. Of course the gentle chime of a church bell was missing, but that would come later. Before that there was still much to do to organise the peace and well-being of the hundred families freed at last from the robber landlords.

He opened the door and the first thing he saw were two bodies huddled under the blanket on the camp-bed. Only the dog deigned to open an eye, and he shut it again at once with a grunt of contentment. A wave of happiness flooded through the Guardian Angel and it was so strong that for a moment he could not move from the doorway.

Since the prodigal son had come back of his own accord, it showed that he had for Bois-Bréau the same affection which brought two kindly souls back each morning to its poverty-stricken doors. Now there would be three of them, for the young wanderer had the same gift of cheerfulness which helps to cure the sick and comfort the afflicted.

181

A little later Cady awoke to the smell of hot coffee. The cups were already set on the surgery table, and the Guardian Angel was stirring his to melt the sugar. They grinned like a couple of conspirators before either of them spoke.

'Where have you been?' the man of God asked at last. 'You don't have to tell me if you don't want to.'

'Big-game hunting out Argenteuil way until nightfall. Around noon word went round the village that the Mangler had got away.'

'Did you catch him?'

'He gave me quite a job. Then I took him to a place where he'll be much better guarded than if he were in prison—the shanty-town of La Frette. Bois-Bréau is a paradise compared with that place!'

The Guardian Angel was only listening with half an ear.

'Why did you come back?'

There was a look in his eye which made Cady think hard. To be honest, he had gone off hoping to come across the Scrap-metal King in his journeyings, but without any intention of ever coming back.

'I didn't want to hurt you,' he muttered. 'You taught me something which no one had ever told me about, not even old Augustine, and she was a good woman, whatever you say.'

'And what was it?'

'I don't know. I haven't the words to say what it is. But when I happen to think about it, all of a sudden I'm happy and I can see that lamp alight in the darkness. That's why I came back.'

'The gipsies' lamp lights nothing which you can see in the Green House. It's just a sign that the other evening a spring started to flow under the floorboards which the Mangler leased to us at so high a rent. The water comes from far away. It's warm in winter and cool in summer, always sweet, and it quenches the thirst of all who drink. The miracle is that it should ever have sprung up in this den of thieves.'

'But for them,' Cady observed, 'perhaps it might never have flowed so swiftly into the shanty-town.'

'You're right. And the evil they did is almost forgotten. All that they have left behind is the well of goodness which they dug in Bois-Bréau, unaware of what they were doing, because the people here had grown so wretched.'

Cady liked the picture which he had painted.

'The thieves' well . . . '

'Drink!' The Guardian Angel handed him his cup. 'From now on things are going to get better and better.'